Sparks seemed to be coming from Lorenzo's eyes. "I don't think I'm the one who needs to prove anything. I think that's for you to do."

"What exactly do you think I need to prove? That you don't bother me?" Altitude sickness on the second floor—that was Sophy's problem. She must be the world's first case, but she'd swear the air was thinner here, because she could hardly get her words higher than a whisper.

His brows flickered. "Don't I?"

Possibly the only librarian who got told off for talking too much, **NATALIE ANDERSON** decided writing books might be more fun than shelving them—and, boy, is it that! Especially writing romance—it's the realization of a lifetime dream kick-started by many an afternoon spent devouring Grandma's Harlequin romances....

She lives in New Zealand, with her husband and four gorgeous-but-exhausting children. Swing by her website any time—she'd love to hear from you: www.natalie-anderson.com.

REBEL WITH A CAUSE

NATALIE ANDERSON

~ MAVERICK MILLIONAIRES ~

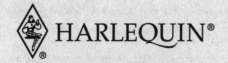

HARLEQUIN®

TORONTO • NEW YORK • LONDON
AMSTERDAM • PARIS • SYDNEY • HAMBURG
STOCKHOLM • ATHENS • TOKYO • MILAN • MADRID
PRAGUE • WARSAW • BUDAPEST • AUCKLAND

Recycling programs
for this product may
not exist in your area.

ISBN-13: 978-0-373-52804-2

REBEL WITH A CAUSE

Previously published in the U.K. under the title
UNBUTTONED BY HER MAVERICK BOSS

First North American Publication 2011

Copyright © 2010 by Natalie Anderson

Printed in U.S.A.

REBEL WITH A CAUSE

Kathleen Anderson, Kath Hadfield, Grandma. Twenty years have passed since you left us, but you know I still have your library of M&B— and I'm adding my own to it now. Wish you were here so I could show you. But I know you know, and you know you live on in our hearts. Always will. Thank you for giving me the belief in everlasting love.

CHAPTER ONE

TIME stood still for no man. And Sophy Braithwaite didn't stand still either.

She tapped her toes on the concrete floor. Slowly at first, just releasing a smidge of the energy pushing under her skin, but after a while the small rapping sound sped up.

The receptionist had directed her straight up the stairs to the office—the sign on the door ensured she'd found the one the woman meant. So she was in the right place at the right time.

Waiting.

She turned and studied the pictures on the wall beside her. Picturesque scenes of Italian countryside—she figured they were Cara's choice. Her assessment and appreciation took less than a minute. Then she looked again at the monstrosity masquerading as the desk. Good thing she wasn't into corporate espionage or fraud. She'd had ample time to rifle through files for sensitive info. Mind you, given the mess it was in, she wouldn't even find anything as useful as a pen in there. The papers were piled high in dangerously unstable towers. The unopened mail had long since filled the in-tray and now cascaded across the computer keyboard. Cara hadn't been exaggerating when she'd said she'd left it in a mess. If anything she'd been understating the case.

'I've just not had my head there and it all got away from me. I feel so terrible now with this happening,' she'd said.

'This' was the early arrival of her baby. Six weeks premature, the tiny sweetie was still in hospital and Cara was hollow-eyed and anxious. The last thing she needed was to be worrying about the part-time admin job she did for a local charity.

Sophy's irritation with the situation spiked. Where was he, then? This Lorenzo Hall—supposed hotshot of the wine industry and darling of the fundraising divas—the CEO of this chaos?

'Lorenzo's so busy at the moment. With Alex and Dani away he's dealing with everything on his own.' Cara had sounded so concerned for him when Sophy's sister, Victoria, had handed the phone to her. 'It would be just brilliant if you could go in there and stop him worrying about the Whistle Fund at least.'

Well, Sophy wasn't here to stop Lorenzo Hall from worrying, she was here to stop Cara worrying.

She realised she'd been subconsciously tapping in time to a rhythmic thunking sound coming from a distance. As if someone were using a hammer or something but speeding up, then stopping, then starting again. She shook her head free of the annoyance and looked around at the chaos again. It would take a bit of time to sort through. She wished she could say no. But then, she never said no. Not when someone asked for help like this. And didn't they all know it. She'd arrived back in New Zealand less than a month ago, yet her family had managed to fill her schedule to bursting already. But she'd let them, passively agreeing to it all. So much for becoming more assertive and ring fencing even just *some* time for her own work.

She knew they saw no change, and wasn't she acting as if there weren't—with her 'yes, of course' here and 'sure' there? Tacitly acknowledging she had nothing better to do. Or, at least, nothing as important as what they were asking.

But she did.

While she loved to help them out, there was something else she loved to do. Her heart beat faster as she thought of it as 'work'. She badly wanted to prove it could be just that. But to make a go of it, she needed time.

So she really didn't want to be standing here waiting for anybody—certainly not some guy who couldn't even seem to organise his own temp. The same boss who had Cara calling her from her hospital bed asking if she could help out. If her help really was needed, then okay, but she wasn't going to wait here for another twenty minutes. She glanced at her watch again. Ordinarily looking at it brought a tingle of pleasure—fine little vintage piece that it was. She'd found it in a flea market in South London one day. With a new old strap she'd found at another market and a trip to the watch doctor, it worked beautifully. It was definitely not running fast.

The thudding impinged into her brain again, stirring a dormant memory from school days.

No. Surely not?

She stood, walked across the office and right round behind the desk to the window. Looked straight down to the asphalt yard at the back of the warehouse. She inhaled some much-needed cool air into her lungs.

But *yes.* Basketball.

Lorenzo Hall—she just knew it was him—out there having himself some fun. If he'd been playing with even

one other person she might have understood it—that he'd
wanted to finish the game before seeing her. But there was
no opponent to beat. He was playing alone—while she was
waiting for a scheduled meeting with him. Long minutes
up in his office—and it was for *his* benefit.

The irritation rose to a rolling boil. How come no one
realised her time was precious too? She walked out of the
office, her high heels clipping quickly down the stairs. She
passed the receptionist, who was running in the other direction with the cord of her phone headset trailing after her.

'Will Mr Hall be long, do you think?' Sophy asked with
extreme politeness.

The receptionist stopped, but looked harassed. 'He's not
up there?'

Sophy gave the woman a cool stare. She didn't know?
Wasn't she his receptionist? Where was the efficiency in
this place—off on a holiday to Mars? She inhaled and
crisped up even more. 'Obviously not.'

The frown on the receptionist's face deepened. 'I'm sure
I saw him earlier. You could look and see if he's up on the
third floor or try out the back.' With that she was gone,
hurrying to do whatever it was that was so urgent.

Sophy continued down the stairs and went through
the doorway behind Reception. This was a meeting that
had been arranged two days ago. He might be the newly
crowned king of the wine exporters, but for the life of her
she couldn't figure out how he'd managed it. Not when he
couldn't even make it to a meeting on time. She found what
had to be the door leading out to the yard. She paused for a
second, squared her shoulders and then turned the handle,
pulling the heavy wood back.

From what she'd seen at the window upstairs she'd
known what she was about to face—but she hadn't ac-

counted for the effect it would have on her up close. She swallowed, momentarily speechless.

He had his back to her—a mightily broad back it was too, and very bronzed. Well, it would be from all the time he obviously spent out here—*shirtless*.

The fire that blazed through her was surely all due to anger.

The baseboard and basket were on a stand on the far side of the asphalt square. He had the ball in hand, feet apart, his knees slightly bent as he readied to take the shot.

Sophy waited for the exact moment. Just as his body moved to shoot the ball, she called—raising her normal volume more than a fraction, and using what her speech and drama teacher had referred to as 'the tone'.

'Lorenzo Hall?'

Needless to say, he didn't make the basket. Sophy smiled. But then, in an instant, it died on her lips.

Even with the three or so metres between them she could feel the scorching heat of him. He turned his head, looked her over—a quick, slicing glance with the darkest eyes she'd ever seen. Then he turned back to the wretched basket.

That had been all he needed to sum her up? Sophy wasn't used to being dismissed so quickly. She might not have lived up to her family's stellar success in the legal fraternity, but she did okay in the appearance stakes. Always immaculate. Always appropriate. Presentation had been drilled into her for so long it was second nature now. So she knew she looked more than acceptable in her baby-blue linen skirt and pressed white shirt. Her lipstick was muted but smooth and her face wasn't shiny. Her one-style-only hair would be in place—she didn't even have to try for that to happen.

The ball had bounced a couple of times. He barely had

to move to retrieve it. Once it was back in his broad hands he turned and gave her another look—even more pointed. Then he turned back to face the baseboard, took careful aim and replayed the shot—landing it this time.

Sophy would have turned and walked if she wasn't too angry to move. So that was the way of it, huh? His little game of by-myself-basketball was more important than a meeting scheduled with her. She'd heard nothing but positives about this guy's charitable organisation. Had heard the rumours about his own background and his meteoric rise—marvellous, wasn't it, people said, that someone with a background like that could become such a success?

Well, Sophy wasn't about to patronise the selfish jerk. 'Are we meeting any time soon?' She *refused* to offer to come back at another time—bit back the conciliatory words by pushing her jaws together. She wasn't going to put herself out at all for him.

The ball had bounced back to him again. He tossed it to the side and walked towards her. His jeans sat low on his hips. He wore them with no belt and she saw a glimpse of a waistband—briefs or boxers? She shouldn't be wondering. But she couldn't stop looking.

There was no fat beneath his skin, just lithe muscles that rippled as he walked. She managed to force her gaze a fraction higher, skimming over the dusting of masculine hair, the dark nipples. He had straight, broad shoulders. Sleek curving muscles stretched down his arms. And all over was the sheen of sweat—burnishing the smooth, sun bronzed skin.

She found she was mirroring his slight breathlessness. His chest was rising and falling that bit quickly, that bit jerkily, and her own felt tight as she studied him. He had an amazing torso—the strength, the undeniable masculinity had her spellbound. Her gaze coasted downwards again.

He took two more steps—bringing him too close. Startled, she looked up as he loomed over her. Realised that with a narrowed, keen gaze he was watching the way she was looking him up and down.

She met his stare, matched it, refusing to let her embarrassment at being caught ogling burn her skin red. But then, when he knew he had her attention, he let his gaze strip down every inch of her body. She actually *felt* the way his attention lit on her neck, on the small V of exposed skin on her chest, on the curve of her breasts...

She fought harder to stop the blush and felt her anger resurge. But she probably deserved it. Hadn't she just done this to him? But not intentionally—not *provocatively*. She just hadn't realised quite how obvious she'd been or how long she'd been staring—her brain had gone AWOL while her eyes feasted.

But his was a deliberate, blatantly sexual action.

Her toes curled in the tips of her heeled pumps. The rest of her wanted to shrivel too—so she could disappear. And she used the anger to block that other message striving to move from brain to body—the desire that wanted to unfurl and scurry through her veins.

'You must be Sophy.' He gestured back to his mini basketball court. 'I was thinking. Lost track of time.'

Well, that fell way too short for an apology.

'My time is valuable to me,' she asserted vocally for the first time in her life. 'I don't like it being wasted.'

Certainly not by a half naked man. Not like this anyway.

Those black, bottomless eyes met hers. The colour rose a little higher on his cheekbones. She wasn't sure if it was from exertion, embarrassment or anger. She suspected the latter.

'Of course,' he said smoothly—too quietly. 'I won't do it again.'

Something had kindled in his eyes as he'd added that. Something she didn't care to define. As it was she felt herself flushing—unable to stop it now—as if she were the one in the wrong. She shifted her weight from one foot to the other. Stole another quick glance at his torso and then aimed to concentrate on the concrete.

'You never seen a man sweat before, Sophy?' His soft question hit her in the gut.

The crisp spring morning suddenly got a whole lot hotter. She tried to say something. Couldn't. The dry irony in his voice just devastated her.

He turned away from her. 'Want to play a little one on one?' he asked. 'I find it helps me focus. You might find it helps you too.'

Oh, so she needed help with focus? Heaven help her she did.

'It's also good for burning excess energy.'

Now *that* was said with deliberate innuendo. He was trying to tip her balance—as if he weren't doing it already with his sheer physicality which was on display. With considerable effort she pulled herself together. Well, she could do a little innuendo too. His few words could flame, but her cool delivery would crush. 'I'm obviously overdressed.'

His eyes widened fractionally, before he replied calmly, 'Easily fixed.'

She lifted her brows very slowly, determined to stay cool. 'You want me to strip?'

He laughed then, his whole face breaking into an absolute charmer of a smile. Sophy lifted her fingers to her mouth to stop her jaw from gaping in surprise. His whole demeanour changed—like quicksilver—from seriously brooding to sparkling good humour. The flash was utterly intriguing and devastatingly attractive.

'It would be fair, don't you think?' he said. 'I mean, you have me at a disadvantage.'

'You put yourself at a disadvantage.' She was even more breathless now. And privately she thought his semi-nudity a huge benefit to him—how to fuzzle the minds of your business opponents in one easy step. She angled away from him—trying to recover her equilibrium. She got a clear view of the fence and saw one section was covered with a huge bit of graffiti. The colours leapt out, almost 3D, in bold blocks. An image of a man—like an ancient statue— with vibrant shades of blue leaping out from behind and an indecipherable word shooting up from one side. She'd never have expected it; the reception area she'd walked through had been incredibly slick—it was only the office upstairs that had been a total mess. Now there was this— what many people would consider an eyesore.

He walked in front of her line of vision and picked up the ball again, spinning it in his hands. 'We can talk through the details at the same time.'

He was still smiling but there was an edge back now—a deliberate challenge. But it was one she just had to turn down. No way was she playing ball with him. This wouldn't be like some Hollywood movie where she scored a hoop first shot. She'd miss it by a mile and totally embarrass herself. She hadn't played in years—to land baskets you needed to practise. She had no hope of relying on muscle memory now.

'Perhaps it would be best if we reschedule this meeting,' she ducked it.

The smile tugged harder on one corner of his mouth.

'You might want to take a shower now,' she added coldly.

His brows lifted then. 'You really don't like sweat?'
He laughed as he looked over her pale blue suit. 'No. You
wouldn't, would you?'

She went silent—refusing to rise to that one. Truth was,
she was feeling utterly human right now and starting to
sweat herself just from looking at him. Cara hadn't mentioned that her boss was completely gorgeous.

She looked at the graffiti again, eyes narrowed as she
tried to work out one of the letters in that word.

'Damn kids.' He'd followed the direction of her gaze.

'It could be worse,' she said. Not wanting to find anything to agree on with him.

'You think?'

'Yeah, it could just be a tag—you know, initials, a name
or something. But that's actually quite a cool picture.'

He coughed. It started as a clear-your-throat kind of
cough, but rapidly turned into a hacking one that sounded
as if he were in danger of losing a lung. Anyone else and
she'd ask if he was okay. But she wasn't going anywhere
nearer the personal with him. As it was they'd crossed
some polite lines already and she was finding it way too
unsettling.

'It must have taken a while.' She commented more on
the graffiti just to cover the moment until he breathed freely
at last. There actually was a lot of depth to the design. It
couldn't possibly be a three-minute spray and run number.
'But it's bad to do it to someone else's property.'

'You're so right.'

She gave him a quick look. Was that a touch of laughter
in his voice? His expression was back to brooding, even
so, she suspected him.

'So you're desperate for an administrator, is that right?'
Finally she snapped back on track.

'For the Whistle Fund, yes.' He too suddenly went professional. 'Kat, my receptionist here, has been too busy to be able to help much since Cara left. We've got a lot on right now so I need someone who can stay on board for at least a month. I need the mess sorted and then help with training a new recruit. I haven't even got to advertise yet. Can you commit to it?' He looked serious. 'You'll be paid of course. I wouldn't expect anyone to take on this level of work voluntarily.'

'I don't need to be paid. I like to work voluntarily.'

'You'll be paid,' he clipped. 'You can donate it back to the charity if you like, but you'll be paid.'

So he didn't want to be beholden to her? But she didn't need the money, the income from her trust fund was more than enough for her to get by. She'd always needed something to give her a sense of dignity—had never sat around doing nothing but shopping and socialising. It wasn't the way she'd been raised. Yes, they had money, but they still had to do something worthwhile with their time. Only she hadn't managed to follow in the family footsteps and pursue a law based career. Her mother, brother and sister were all super successful lawyers. All the true save-the-oppressed kind, not corporate massive-fee-billing sharks. Worse was her father, who was a retired judge. He still worked—publishing research, heading reviews of the system. Sophy's surname was synonymous with excellence in the field. Not one of them had failed or even deviated from that path.

Only Sophy.

So she'd tried to gain her credibility by being the yes-person. Doing all the voluntary stuff, being the consummate organiser of everything they asked for—mainly their own lives. She might not have their legal brains, but she was practical. Yet in trying to keep up with them she'd made one stupid, massive mistake—she'd mistaken her personal value. So she'd gone away. While overseas she'd finally found her own passion, her own calling. And as soon as she got the time she was going to build her business and prove her skill to the family.

'Cara's office is in the building here.' He seemed to take her silence for acquiescence. 'It's all yours. I thought we could cover her okay but with her baby coming so soon and with Dani away with Alex, I need someone who can concentrate wholly on it.'

'Full time?' Sophy's heart was sinking. She just wasn't going to be able to say no.

'Maybe for the first week to catch up.' His grin was touchingly rueful. 'After that just the mornings should be enough. And I'd need you to be present at whatever evening meetings there are and the functions. Actually, you need to finalise the details for the next one.'

Yes. The Whistle Fund was famous for its functions—fabulous evenings of entertainment that drew the rich and famous out, and got them to open their wallets too. The presence of the 'stars' meant the presence of Joe Public was huge too—everybody liked to be a VIP for a night.

'You can't find anyone else?' Sophy tried one last avenue. 'Maybe from a temp agency?'

'Cara wanted to be sure the office was in good hands. She doesn't trust that a stranger will be able to come in and fix it. I don't want to stress her any more than she already is. And she told me you're the only one who can get this job done. I promised her I'd give you a shot.'

Sophy's ears pricked at the slight hint of sarcasm—did he think she couldn't get it done? Her spine stiffened—why, she could sort that lot upstairs in her sleep.

Cara had pleaded for her to come. Because Sophy's sister, Victoria, was one of Cara's best friends. And Victoria had talked to Cara—assured her Sophy was the one to do it: she was available, she was capable. Now it seemed she was all Cara could accept.

Sophy might as well have never gone away. Since landing back she'd stepped straight back into the overcommitted, overscheduled life she'd left two years before. No one had stopped to think she might have other things she wanted to do. And why should they? Hadn't she been saying yes—as she always had?

So she should say no now. Say sorry, but that she had other priorities and couldn't give him that much time. She looked at him, tried really hard not to let her gaze slip down his body again. There was a hard look in his eyes—as if he didn't really believe what Cara had told him about her, and that he expected her to say no. That he'd just as soon phone for some anonymous temp and be done with it. Suddenly she sensed that he didn't like having to ask her at all. That made her stand up even straighter.

And there was Cara herself, wasn't there? Hovering over her tiny daughter in the incubator—with enough on her mind without needlessly worrying about her boss being so stressed out. What a crock. If Cara had seen him today, she'd have known she had no cause for concern—he was so relaxed he was out wasting time playing ball. But Sophy couldn't let her sister's friend down—just as she'd never let her sister down.

'I'll be back tomorrow to start,' she said briskly.

'I'll be here to show you the ropes.'

'Nine a.m.' She let her gaze rake him one last time. 'Sharp.'

She turned and walked. His words came just as the door closed behind her. Whether she was meant to hear the low suggestively spoken reply she didn't know, but she did—and it almost incinerated her.

'Yes, ma'am.'

CHAPTER TWO

NINE a.m. came and went. Sophy sat in the office that looked as if it had been hit by a cyclone and checked her watch every thirty seconds or so. Unbelievable. No wonder this place was in such a mess. He certainly needed help. But he was so going the wrong way about getting it.

She filled in five minutes by moving some of the mail to find the keyboard. Decided to start opening and sorting it. Forty minutes later a portion of the desk was clear, the recycling bin was full of envelopes and half the letters were neatly stacked in classified piles. At that point she decided she shouldn't go further without consulting him. She went downstairs to the receptionist.

'Kat? I'm Sophy. Here to work on the Whistle Fund admin. Do you know where Mr Hall is?'

The receptionist blinked at her. 'I thought he was up with you. I've been taking messages because he's not picking up the phone.'

'Well, he's not with me.'

'He's not out the back?'

No. Naturally out of the window had been the first place she'd looked. Sophy heard the front doors slide open and turned expectantly. A courier driver walked in with a parcel under his arm.

'Can you see if he's on the third floor?' Kat asked. 'I need to deal with this.'

'Of course,' Sophy answered automatically.

The third floor—was that where Lorenzo's office was? She climbed the stairs. Stopped at the second floor and checked the other two offices there once more—both were in a far better state than Cara's. They actually looked as if people worked in them—several people even—but there was no one present. Further along the corridor there was a massive room that was almost totally empty. Was the place run by ghosts? The communication was appalling. Sophy swallowed the flutter of nerves as she climbed up the next flight of stairs. There was no corridor off them this time—just the one door marked 'private'.

She knocked. No answer.

She knocked again. Still no answer.

Without thinking about it she tried the handle. The door swung open and she stepped inside.

The space was huge—and much brighter than the dimly lit stairwell. Sunlight shone through the skylight windows in the roof. She blinked rapidly and took in the scene. This wasn't office space. This was an apartment—*Lorenzo's* apartment.

And if she wasn't mistaken, the sofa was occupied.

'What's wrong?' Pure instinct drove her forward to where he was sprawled back on the wide sweep of leather.

It was hard dragging her eyes up his chest to his face but once she did she was able to focus better. Beneath the tan he was pale, but dark shadows hung under his eyes. Hell, if this was a hangover she'd be so mad with him.

'Sore throat.' A total croak, not the slight rasp of yesterday.

Sore throat and then some, Sophy reckoned. He looked

dreadful. Actually he didn't, he looked one shade less than magnificent. So that meant he really must be sick. She couldn't help give him the once over again. Just impossible not to when he had the most amazing body she'd ever seen up close.

He was in boxers—nothing but boxers. Not the loose fitting pure cotton kind, but the knit type that clung to his slim hips, muscled thighs—and other intriguing bits.

So that was that question answered. And a few others too.

Sophy stopped her gaping. She needed to pull herself together and deal with him.

'You have a temperature.' It was obvious from his glistening skin. She marched to the kitchen area in the open-plan space. Poured a glass of water. Wished she could snatch a moment to drink one herself, but she was too concerned about how feverish he looked.

'I'm fine.' He coughed, totally hacking up that lung.

'Of course you are,' Sophy said smartly. 'That's why you missed our meeting.' She held out the glass to him. His hand shook as he reached for it. She took his fingers and wrapped them round the glass herself. Only when certain he had it did she let him go.

Their eyes met when she looked up from the glass. She saw the raw anger in his—impotent anger.

'I'm fine,' he repeated, grinding the words through his teeth.

Yeah, right. He was shivering. He ditched the water on the coffee table in front of the sofa after only the tiniest sip. His laptop was on the table too, the faintest hum coming from it. Did he really think he was capable of work?

'When did you last eat?' she asked, her practical nature asserting itself.

He winced.

'I need to take your temperature.'

'Rot.'

She gingerly placed her palm on his forehead. Snatched it away at the same time that he jerked back.

'Quit it,' he said hoarsely.

She curled her tingling fingers. 'You're burning up. You need to see a doctor.'

'Rubbish.'

'Not negotiable.' Sophy pulled her mobile from her pocket and flipped it open. 'I can get someone to come here.'

'Don't you dare.' It would have sounded good if his voice hadn't cracked in the middle. He tried to move, evidently thought better of it and just rasped bitterly, 'Sophy, back off. I'm fine. I have work I need to get on with.'

She ignored him, spoke to the receptionist at the clinic she'd been to all her life. Two minutes later she hung up. 'A locum will be here in ten.'

'Too bad. I'm not seeing him. I have to do this—'

'Your social networking will have to wait.' Sophy closed the laptop. Picked it up and put it far, far away on the kitchen bench.

'Bring that back here—I was working.'

She went close and looked down at him. 'I really wish I had one of those old-fashioned mercury thermometers. I know where I'd stick it.'

'Don't.' His hand shot out and gripped her wrist—hard. 'You're right. I'm not feeling well. And if you keep provoking me I'll snap.'

Really? And do what?

She stared into dark eyes, saw the tiredness, the strain, the frustration—and even deeper she saw the unhappiness. At that she relented. 'Okay. But you have to stop fighting me too. You're sick, you need to see a doctor and you need taking care of.'

He shifted on the sofa.

'Look, it's happening whether you agree or not, Lorenzo. Why not make it that bit more pleasant?'

He breathed in—she could see the effort hurting him. He closed his eyes and she knew she'd won. 'Okay, but you've done your thing. You can go now. Kat can send the doctor up.' Another tremor shook him.

But she didn't think she could go now. She couldn't leave anyone alone in this state. And oddly enough she felt that even more strongly about him—he'd never admit it, but he was vulnerable. He was alone.

He shook his head slightly and looked cheesed again. 'At least bring my laptop back.'

'What's the point, Lorenzo?' she said quietly. 'Staring at the screen isn't going to get it done. You're better off getting some sleep and getting well. Then you'll do the work in a quarter of the time.'

His head fell back against the sofa cushions. Round two to her.

The doctor stayed only ten minutes. Sophy waited on the top of the stairs, put her phone in action some more. Then, after exchanging a few words with the doctor on her way out, she went back in to face the grumpy patient.

'I'm getting you a rug,' she said, heading towards the doors at the back of the room, refusing to be embarrassed about the idea of going into his bedroom.

'There's one on the end of the sofa.'

She stopped. So there was. She'd not noticed it. Hard to notice anything else in the room when he was mostly naked. 'Well—' she tried not to stare at him as she reached down and picked it up '—I think perhaps you'd better put it on. You don't want to get a chill.'

He was well enough to send her an ironic glance. But he leaned back on the sofa and pulled the rug over his waist and down his legs. 'Happy now, nursie?'

His chest was still bare, so, no, she wasn't. But he was obviously feeling a touch better. The doctor said she'd given him some pain relief—must be fast acting stuff.

'So it's tonsillitis?' Sophy asked carefully, not wanting to intrude too much, yet unable to stop.

'Stupid, isn't it?' Lorenzo said.

No. Like anyone, Sophy knew how painful a sore throat could be. 'Did you get it as a child?'

'A bit.' He nodded. 'Haven't had it in years, though.'

'They didn't take them out for you?' While it might not be a regular practice any more, she knew that for the most recurrent cases they still did tonsillectomies.

He repositioned his head on the sofa cushions again. 'I was on the waiting list for a while. But it never happened. When I got to boarding school the episodes seemed to stop.'

Sophy poured the electrolyte drink the doctor had given her into a glass. 'It was a good school, wasn't it?'

'Better than all the others I went to.'

She knew he'd been at school with Alex Carlisle—his partner in setting up the Whistle Fund. It was the school her elder brother had gone to too—years before. Private, exclusive, incredibly academic and with superior sporting results as well. It was a tough place to shine—and she just knew Lorenzo had shone. Her sister had gone to the girls' equivalent. But by the time Sophy had come along their parents were happy for her to just go to the local—they'd said they didn't want to send her away to board. But Sophy knew it was because she hadn't had the off-the-charts grades her siblings had had. It wasn't that she was below average, she just wasn't brilliant. 'The antibiotics will have you better in no time. Then maybe you should have a holiday.'

His brows shot up.

'Cara says you've been working too hard,' Sophy said blandly, ignoring his mounting outrage. 'Perhaps you've gotten run down.' At that she sent him a look from under her lashes—unable to resist the temptation to let a hint of flirt out.

'Honey, I'm hardly run down.' His muscles rippled as he stretched out his arms in an unabashed display of male preening.

Oh, he was definitely feeling better. And she just couldn't resist teasing him some more.

'The muscles might look good, Lorenzo,' the devil made her whisper, 'but you wouldn't be up to it. You'd be spent just trying to stand.'

'You want to move closer and we'll test that out?' Sick or not, he didn't miss a beat.

She turned and paced away. Enough channelling of Rosanna—Sophy just wasn't as practised a flirt as her best friend. 'I'm not in the mood for more disappointments.'

'You were disappointed I wasn't there to meet you?'

She spun and caught his amused, *satisfied* look. She inhaled. 'You should be lying down. Hurry up and finish that drink.'

'Sophy—' his eyes glittered '—I don't need a mother.' It was a slicing rejection of any sort of kindness.

'No,' she agreed curtly. 'You need a nurse. I've arranged for one to come from an agency.'

Lorenzo was so shocked he couldn't speak for a full minute. He repeated her words in his head several times. Still didn't believe it. 'You've *what*?'

'I've got a nurse coming. I've got work to get on with, so does Kat, and you can't be left alone.'

Can't be left alone? What did she think he'd been all his life? 'You can tell your nurse she's not necessary.'

'No. Too late for that.' She moved back to the table and took away the empty glass. 'She's on her way.'

Oh, she thought she was so damn competent, didn't she? 'She'll have a mobile. Call it.' Wasn't getting a doctor around enough for this woman? Another tremor shook him from the bones out. Blow the fever—he was boiling mad.

'Don't bother trying, Lorenzo,' she said coolly, cutting him off before he'd even got started. 'She's on her way and she's staying.'

He gritted his teeth and glared at her. He'd never felt this frustration—hadn't felt this useless since he was a kid being shunted from place to place with no say in it.

He closed his eyes as a wave of utter weariness hit him. Okay, he had been working hard—even harder than usual recently. He didn't know when his hunger for success would be filled. Always he was chased by the feeling that it could be whisked away from him, that he'd wake up one day and find himself with nothing. So he worked, worked, worked—building the base bigger. He could never have enough of the security he needed.

But investing in Vance's bar idea might have been one project too many. He'd sent all his staff and resources there for the last week. Helping him get ready for the big opening night—which Lorenzo was going to miss at this rate. As a result his own offices had been sadly neglected. The Whistle Fund in particular. It wouldn't take too much to get it right again, but it needed time that he simply didn't have right now. He'd been working twenty-hour days in the last fortnight as it was. So Cara's office was a mess. It was stupid, but there was a big part of him that hated this woman seeing it like that.

Sophy—the supremely interfering piece of efficiency.

And how could he be finding her remotely attractive? She was so damn quick and proper and *right* it was nauseating. Had she ever made a mistake in her life? He so didn't think so. And if she had, he bet she'd never admit to it.

Utterly perfect, wasn't she?

He shifted under the rug. She *was* perfect—like a porcelain doll. Creamy skin and a blonde bob that sprang into neat curls at the ends—how long did it take her to get it to sit just so? Then there was that little nose and the lips that had a sweet cupid's bow that begged to be kissed. And big blue eyes that went even bigger when she looked at him—a blend of intense interest and reserve. She looked as if she wanted but was wary. She half teased and then withdrew again. It made him want to pounce all the more. He saw her gaze flick over him again. Damn the weakness in his bones. Because that look in her eyes made him want to strip her bare—inch by beautiful inch—and find out whether the hint of the fire he could see really was just the glow from an inferno beneath. He sure as hell was fantasising it was.

Only he was so damn helpless.

That one last part of his body refused to acknowledge the sickness. He raised his knees, lifting the rug to hide the evidence, and mentally berated himself. So inappropriate. It must be the fever putting these kinds of thoughts into his head.

He looked at her, she was speaking briskly into her phone again. Some other poor soul was at the mercy of her efficiency. He was beyond even trying to listen. All he wanted was to rip the gadget from her and press his mouth to hers—just to shut her up. Just to slake the lust.

So damn irresistible. So damn impossible. For one thing he was harbouring a million nasty bugs in his throat, for another she just wasn't his type. Not at all. Not when he was on form.

But he felt an almost feral need to touch her—had done since the second he'd first seen her looking so snippy out the back of the warehouse. He wanted to muss her up so bad he wanted to growl.

Sick. He really was sick.

'Okay, that's everything settled, then.'

'You're going?' Oh, man. He grimaced. Where had that sound of disappointment come from?

She paused. 'You didn't think I was going to stay, did you? I've got other things to do. And you said it yourself, Lorenzo—you don't need a mother, or any kind of sympathy.'

'So you're going to leave me here at the mercy of some stranger?' He opted to try to wheedle. Thinking on it, he'd rather have her here than some nurse—even if she was a little too efficient for his liking. Did she never stop and slow down? She should slow down—he'd make her. Give it to her really, really slow. Bend her back and lick all the way up her gorgeous length until she... *Hell*, his eyes were probably glazing over. He shut them tight. It made the fantasy worse. It made the aching in his gut worse.

On seconds thoughts, the sooner Sophy left, the better.

'She's very well qualified and has great references,' Sophy said—oblivious to the base nature of his thoughts. 'She'll get you right again.'

'I do not need a damn nursemaid.' What was she going to do all day? He'd had the pills, now he just needed to sleep until it was time to take more. The last thing he wanted was some woman poking round his apartment. He never let women poke around. He liked his privacy—the peace in isolation.

'Your temperature is sky-high. Until it's down and the antibiotics have kicked in, then you are not being left alone. We're talking twenty-four hours or less, Lorenzo. Get over it.'

He opened his mouth. Shut it again. He hadn't been given orders quite like that in *years*.

'Now you need to rest. The nurse will be here in twenty. She's bringing more medicine with her.'

Enough was enough. He wasn't putting up with this for a moment longer. He put his feet on the ground and hauled himself up.

'Lorenzo.' Sophy's heart lurched. She moved fast.

His eyes were closed and the frown on his face was heightened by his extreme pallor. His whole body was covered in a film of sweat but he shivered again. She wrapped her arm around him—felt every single muscle in his body go tense. Sophy bit her lip. The sooner the nurse got here, the better.

'I'm fine.' The anger surged in his voice. Directed at both her and himself. He was furious with his weakness.

'And I'm the Queen of Atlantis.'

'This is ridiculous. I'm hardly at death's door. It's a sore throat.' But he sat back down all the same, put his feet up this time and scrunched more into the sofa, lying shivering beneath the rug. His teeth were tightly clenched—to stop them chattering or because he was so mad? Probably both.

Sophy was definitely staying 'til the nurse arrived now. She sat in the chair across from the sofa. Keeping a wary eye on him and sneaking interested glances round his apartment. The space was gorgeous—huge and light.

The kitchen was modern—had all the lovely stainless steel appliances a gourmet home cook could ever want. There was a massive shelving system on one wall—filled with books, CDs, DVDs. She leaned close to look at the titles, even though she knew she was being nosy.

She glanced at her watch. Shouldn't be long now 'til the nurse arrived. He'd gone very quiet. Was he asleep? Quietly she moved back to the sofa, bent so she could see his face.

His jet-black hair was just slightly too long—as if he'd missed his last appointment with the barber—and right now it was a tousled mess. It was gorgeous—just begging for fingers to tunnel into it. And his features were beautiful. His eyelashes were annoyingly long while the shadow on his angular cheek tempted her to touch. And then there was his mouth. In the heart of his chiselled jaw were the most sensual lips she'd ever seen. Full, gently curved, slightly parted as he slept. The shivering seemed to have eased. Had his temperature dropped? She put her palm on his forehead again.

His hand moved fast, clamping round her wrist as his eyes shot open. The brown so deep as to be black, filled with a fire she wasn't sure was purely fever.

She was caught, crouched half over him, unable to move.

His eyes burned into her. 'I told you to quit it.'

But he wasn't holding her hand away from him, instead he pressed her fingers harder to his skin. Afterwards she never knew from where she'd got the audacity, but she spread her fingers, gently stroking them over his damp brow. Smoothing the frown lines, stretching higher to reach into his hair, rumpling it ever so gently.

Her fingertips felt so sensitive—never had she felt something so strong inside from just touching someone. The strangest kind of electricity surged into her. Thrilling yet relaxing at the same time. It felt right to be touching him. It felt good. Okay, more than good. Sexual energy strummed through her, just like that. She wanted to move, to touch more, to shift her hips—tease the ache that had woken deep within.

His eyes didn't leave hers, filled with a look so full of... something. Was it anger or desire or something deeper and darker still?

The buzzing made her jump. Made him grip her even harder—so hard she winced.

'That'll be the nurse,' she muttered.

Despite the illness he had fearsome strength when he wanted to use it.

She finally broke away from his deepening gaze, and pointedly looked at his hand. 'You need to let me go.'

His fingers loosened and she pulled her hand free. Her heart was beating so fast she felt dizzy. Maybe it wasn't tonsillitis that he had. Maybe it was the flu and she'd caught it just like that. She felt as hot as he looked.

She caught a glimpse of herself in a mirror hanging on the wall as she hurried to the door. Yes, the colour in her cheeks was definitely more than the usual. And her eyes looked huge.

The nurse was at least fifty and looked like a total grandma with her specs and cardigan and knitting needles poking out of her bag. She talked like a grandma too—incessant, interested and caring but with an underlying thread of steel.

Sophy smothered her smile as the woman began her no nonsense fussing over Lorenzo. Definitely time to make a move. She needed some space to examine that moment again too.

'I'll phone later,' she said to the nurse.

'Aren't you going to talk to me?' A growl from the sofa.

'You're going to be asleep.' Sophy went even warmer inside when she saw the put out look flash on his face.

But then he started shivering again and the nurse turned to him. 'We need to get you into bed, don't we? I'll go and put some nice fresh sheets on it. No, don't worry, I can find them. You just lie back and relax. Medicine, some pain-killers, something nice and warm to drink. We'll have you better in no time.'

Sophy watched the woman bustle off, finding her way around the place by some kind of special nursing sixth sense. She looked back at Lorenzo; he was looking at the nurse with such loathing that Sophy had to clap her hand over her mouth to stop herself laughing. At her movement his head whipped round and he glared at her. Oh, boy, definitely time to go.

'Sophy.'

Halfway across the room she hesitated.

'Come here.'

Sick as he was, it was a command. And Sophy felt a scarily overwhelming urge to do as he bid. How pathetic— it wasn't as if he could do much if she refused.

'Come here.' Softly spoken again, but it wasn't just a thread of steel in there—it was a whole core. And his magnetism wasn't something she could ignore.

She walked over to him. Even though he was the one lying down, even though she was the one who could leave, somehow the balance of power had changed. In those few minutes when she'd been crouched next to him, stroking him, something had changed completely.

She stopped a little distance away, met the deep, dark gaze a little nervously.

'I want to thank you,' he said quietly.

'It's not necessary.' She felt the blush rising in her cheeks.

Sorting out others was her speciality. She had a family of geniuses who could barely organise what they wanted to make for dinner every night. This was nothing.

He was still looking at her so intensely she wondered what it was he was trying to read. His focus dropped, to her mouth. She swallowed—determined not to give herself away by licking her suddenly desperately dry lips. Her pulse thumped in her ears.

'I'm kissing you. Can you feel it?'

Sophy blinked. Had she just dreamed that? Was that a fantasy moment? Had he really just said that? Like *that*—a purring whisper?

Mind sex. Was that what this was? Because she had to admit she was feeling it—and was desperate to feel more. Okay, *she* was delirious. She really was. Definitely burning up. She licked her lips, not realising she was 'til she was done and they were still tingling with the need for touch—*his* touch. His kiss.

Suddenly he was smiling—that absolutely brilliant smile that had disarmed her so completely yesterday.

She snatched in a breath—her lungs felt as if they were eating fire. 'Get better soon.' And she ran, his low chuckle hard on her heels.

Every time Sophy thought of the expression on his face as she'd left she blushed bodily. And it wasn't without a few nerves that she walked up to the second floor three days later. Lorenzo was back on deck—Kat told her as soon as she arrived. And he was waiting for her in his office. She was to see him as soon as she got there.

Sophy had the feeling it was going to be interesting. He hadn't liked her seeing him so vulnerable. Certainly hadn't liked the way she'd handled it. If she'd learned anything about him from their brief meetings so far, he liked to be the boss. Only she'd overruled him. She suspected he was going to make her pay for that—only the burning question was *how*? In the devastatingly direct way that he'd reclaimed the power in his apartment? By using his way-too-potent sensuality? She totally shouldn't be hoping so. Lorenzo Hall had playboy commitment-phobe stamped all over him—in permanent ink. She took a breath and knocked on his door.

'Just a moment.'

She waited, her nerves stretching tauter with every tiny tick of her watch. What was this pause about—did he want to force her to break point? Because he knew, didn't he? Was all too aware of his effect on her—and on any woman. Why, he'd used it to his advantage in his apartment—a look, a very few words and she was practically in a puddle at his feet. Then she heard him.

'Okay, you can come in now.'

She opened the door and stopped on the threshold. Gaped.

He was standing by the window, had turned to watch as she came in. He was in jeans. But still no shirt. From behind him the light touched his body like an aura giving it a golden glow. It didn't need the emphasis. It was blindingly gorgeous already.

It was as if she were two feet from a launch tower that had just sent a rocket into space—the heat from the blast nearly eviscerating her.

His torso was bronzed, no sheen from sweat this time, but she wanted to see it wet again. Her fingers wanted to slide through the slickness, they wanted to torment him to slickness.

She squeezed her eyes shut. Since when did she have rabid sexual fantasies about a virtual stranger? Such uncontrollable, lusty urges? She blamed it on the sight of all that beautiful skin.

'The first time was a mistake,' she muttered. 'The second you couldn't help.' She opened her eyes and stared some more, watching as he slowly walked until he stood ten inches too far within her personal space. 'This time—'

'Was entirely deliberate.'

CHAPTER THREE

ALL Sophy could hear was the thud, thud, thud of her heart. 'Deliberate?'

He smiled. Such a slow, amused smile she wondered whether the word had actually emerged from her mouth or whether it had just been some sort of scared-animal squeak.

'You seemed to like it,' he said quietly, tiny twin lights dancing in his otherwise incredibly dark eyes.

Like it? Oh, that was the understatement of the century.

She blinked at him. He was so calm. So at ease in his gorgeous skin. So sure of his effect on her—the effect he *definitely* had on any woman—he was that confident. It was enough to slap sense back into her. 'You're definitely feeling better, aren't you?'

'One hundred per cent.'

'Great.' Sophy took a step back into the corridor. 'Then perhaps you'd like to see what I've been doing with sorting out the admin in there.'

'I've seen it. It's looking good. It's very easy to understand the system you're setting up.'

'Oh.' She was deflated—he'd stolen the ball back just like that.

'But we do need to talk about the function coming up.'

He walked out to the corridor after her. 'And I need to show you some of the stuff to update the website. I understand Kat's been helping you a bit when she can?'

'Yes, she's been great.' Sophy tried really hard to keep her concentration on the conversation but it kept sliding down to where his flat abs hit his jeans. *Unbelievable*—both his body and her reaction to it.

'The rest of the team will be back in later today. They've been helping on another project.'

'The bar.' Kat had told her about it. Lorenzo was the backer behind some guy opening up a new bar in the heart of cooldom. And she could totally be professional in the face of this provocation. Sure she could.

'Yes.' He was sounding all serious but his eyes were dancing. 'Shall we go into your office and get on with it?'

She stopped only three paces along. Nope. She couldn't be professional—not like this. 'Do you possibly think that you could put a shirt on?'

A deep, totally pure sound of amusement rumbled out of him. 'It really bothers you.'

'It's inappropriate.' Sophy felt her temperature rising. She wasn't a prude—really she wasn't. But this was just before nine a.m. and they were at *work*. Hell, yes, it bothered her.

'No more inappropriate than you bursting into my apartment and ordering a nurse for me.'

Sophy smiled, feeling a sense of power return. 'Now *that* really bothered *you*, didn't it? Me seeing you like that—in such a weakened state. Did it wound your male pride? Is that why you're showing your muscles again now? Proving your masculine strength?'

'You really think I was weak?' He turned, his big frame took up half the space in the corridor. And then he moved.

Instinctively she retreated—backing up against the wall. But he followed, totally hemming her in. She stuck her chin in the air trying not to feel anxious—or, worse, the lick of anticipation.

Sparks seemed to be coming from his eyes. 'I don't think I'm the one who needs to prove anything. I think that's for you to do.'

'What exactly do you think I need to prove? That you don't bother me?' Altitude sickness on the second floor— that was her problem. She must be the world's first case but she'd swear the air was thinner here because she could hardly get her words higher than a whisper.

His brows flickered. 'Don't I?'

'Of course you do.'

His brows shot higher. What, he hadn't expected honesty?

'You're half naked. *All* the time,' she explained the obvious. 'But it's the inappropriateness that bothers me. Not your actual body.' Oh, great, now she sounded prissy. And not at all honest.

His smile was back showing off his even white teeth. And he was playing with her the way a cat did a mouse. She needed to talk to Rosanna—really badly. She needed advice from a pro. Because there was no way she was letting Lorenzo Hall win this with such one-sided ease. She wasn't going to roll over and be the latest in what she was certain was a very long line—at least not without scoring some points of her own. For nor was she going to cut off her nose to spite her face. She wasn't going to deny herself a moment of pure pleasure should the opportunity arise. Yes, he bothered her—like that. Yes, she wanted him.

But she'd make like Rosanna and have him on her terms. For once in her life she was going to turn her back on responsibility; she'd take a risk and go for something she wanted. She just had to figure out how.

Lorenzo knew he was being naughty. But there was that bit in him that had always derived pleasure from taking risks. From doing exactly what society said he shouldn't—stretching the boundaries as far as he could and stopping only just before they broke.

He had matured—his transgressions were nothing near the edge he'd veered towards all those years ago. He stayed on the right side of the law now. But this oh-so-perfect Miss made him push it. Even just this little bit, to risqué, to rude, when really he wanted to ravish—really, really badly.

The look on her face had been worth the dodgy removal of his shirt. So worth it—even if he was struggling to contain his wayward hormones now. He just wanted to reach out and pull her against him—hard. His skin was on fire—had been since she'd touched him in his apartment the other day. Her small, cool hand hadn't soothed him at all—had only stirred the desire he'd already been battling to control. In those first twenty-four hours when the sickness was at its worst, he'd done nothing but dream of her. He was still dreaming of her and where he wanted that hand.

He'd been working too hard, round the clock with no room for fun. But it should ease up soon. Once the bar was open he'd be able to take a step back. And have some fun. Then again, there was no reason why he couldn't have some fun right now.

Her eyes had narrowed. He could just about see the cogs turning and whirring in her brain. The vixen-with-training-wheels looked as if she was plotting.

A phone rang—hers. Her hand went to her bag. He was disappointed to see her move. But he didn't move away. Took too much pleasure in watching her shrink back an awkward inch as she answered. But felt the pleasure turn to ash when he heard the male tones. He listened as she organised.

'Yes, don't worry, Ted. I'm picking it up on my way home. I'll drop it round before six.'

Who the hell was Ted? Lorenzo waited 'til she said goodbye. Then let the power of silence work its magic.

'That was my brother. Sorry,' she finally said.

He took the phone from her hand and switched it off. 'When you're with me, all your attention is with me.'

Her eyes widened. He watched her swallow.

'On work,' he added, way too late.

He held out her phone for her to take back. Smiling inside as he saw her jerky movements. Yeah, he liked the way he could bother her. Because she really bothered him. He took a careful step away—right now they both needed a minute. 'I'll go get my shirt and then we'll go through the stuff for Whistle, right?'

Sophy poured the entire contents of the ice tray into her glass—not caring that half the blocks fell out onto the bench and skidded onto the floor. She was unbearably hot—Lorenzo putting his shirt on had made no difference. For over an hour she'd suffered—sitting at the desk while he hovered beside her, behind her. Filling in the holes that had appeared in the days when she'd been working without the information only he or Cara could provide. She'd had the rest of the day to recover—but she hadn't succeeded. She gulped down half the glass of water, sagged against the bench, she was so out of her depth.

'Where have you been? I'm only home for half a day and I wanted us to go for a pedicure and—'

Sophy turned, dropping the glass in the sink. 'You're

back!' Thrilled, she ran across the room and hugged her elusive flatmate.

'Okay, you've missed me too.' Rosanna's arms came round her and tightened. Then pushed her away. 'Shirts, doll, we can't crush our shirts.'

Sophy laughed. In the sentence of life, Sophy figured she was like a verb—the action, the one who got things done. Not very exciting perhaps, but necessary. Rosanna, however, was the exclamation mark. The rare beauty that could fill a whole paragraph—a whole room—with excitement. She even looked like one. Always dressed in black, she was a thin streak of long limbs, her glossy dark hair swept in a high ponytail that swung halfway down her back. She was full of vitality, and sheer outrageousness.

'Now where have you been? I landed hours ago and have been lonely ever since and now the taxi to take me back to the airport will be here in ten. What's up with your mobile?'

Sophy walked back to the bench to find and refill her glass. How was she going to explain this one? Rosanna was not going to be impressed. 'I'm doing some admin work.'

Rosanna frowned. 'You've got a job?'

'Only for a few weeks. Their usual administrator's baby arrived sooner than expected.'

'Baby okay?'

'Baby's fine.'

'So why couldn't they get a temp? Why did it have to be you?' Rosanna rolled her eyes. 'Who asked you?'

'Cara, the new mother, is a good friend of Victoria's.'

'Of course she is. Of course you couldn't say no.' Rosanna gave a theatrical sigh as she went to the pantry and pulled out a bottle of wine. 'So where's the job?'

'You heard of the Whistle Fund?'

Rosanna wolf-whistled as she unscrewed the cap of the bottle. 'Alex Carlisle and Lorenzo Hall. Who hasn't heard of them? Alex got married recently and Lorenzo's someone you don't forget. Ever.'

Well, that was true. His image was burned on Sophy's brain, every inch of skin, muscle and pure man.

'Every bit as good as he looks, apparently,' Rosanna drawled.

'You've hooked him?' A hot flash of envy sliced through Sophy.

'No,' Rosanna said, pausing as she poured the crimson wine. 'Not that I'd turn him down. But the one time our paths crossed I didn't even score a second glance.'

'I'm sure that's not true.' Sophy was able to smile again. 'Every man gives you at least four glances.'

'Sweetie-pie.' Rosanna flopped into a chair, giant wine glass in hand. 'No, I've heard he's impossible to catch. Tangles in the nets now and then but always swims free.'

Sophy was quite sure he tangled and then ripped free. 'I think he's a shark.'

'Do you now?' Rosanna giggled—half choking on her wine.

'Absolutely,' Sophy said. 'I think he's far too used to seeing any fish he wants and getting the kill.'

Rosanna held her glass up to the light and with a flick of her wrist let the liquid swirl inside it. 'At the very least you might score some wine.'

Sophy shook her head. 'I don't know that we'll be getting on well enough for that.'

Rosanna tilted her head on the side and appraised Sophy, a sly smile on her lips. 'You're interested.'

'No I'm not.' Sophy lied. And then immediately started to laugh.

Rosanna laughed too. 'Of course you are. We all are. But—' her nose wrinkled '—I don't think he's your type.'

'No?' Sophy felt irrationally put out.

'He *is* a shark,' Rosanna said. 'You need a dolphin.'

'Oh, great. Someone with a big nose.'

'And with a habit of rescuing rather than destroying. It's true.' Rosanna sat up. 'You need a good guy, Soph, someone safe and cuddly, not some dangerous type you couldn't handle.'

'You don't think I could handle him?'

'I know you couldn't.'

'So you've no advice for me?'

Rosanna looked up sharply. 'I'm the last person you should take advice from.'

How did she figure that? She was the one who had them all eating out of her palm.

'You were wearing that when you saw him?' Rosanna's expression clouded.

'What? What's wrong with it?' Had she committed some terrible fashion faux pas? She couldn't think what.

'Nothing. But if he has a Grace Kelly fantasy, then you're in trouble.'

Sophy snorted. 'Now who's the sweetie-pie?'

'He'd gobble a kitten like you.' Rosanna frowned. 'Don't say I didn't warn you. Anyway, I'm grumpy, we don't have time for a pedicure now. I've had to sit here all day doing nothing.'

Kitten? She thought she was a *kitten*? 'Poor you.' Now Sophy had zero sympathy. 'It's about time you stopped and did nothing for half a day.'

Rosanna cupped her hand round her mouth, making a pretend megaphone. 'Pot calling kettle, come in, kettle.' She stood. 'At least I'm busy pushing my career. You're just busy doing everything for everyone else.'

'You're going to miss your next flight. Go have a good trip.' Rosanna was a buyer for one of the major fashion chains. Knowledgeable, chic, damn good at her job and away more nights than she was at home.

Rosanna picked up the handle of her chic trolley case. 'I love Wellington.'

'The boys are going to miss you.'

'It'll be good for them.' Rosanna bent and flicked an invisible speck of fluff from her black trousers.

Sophy watched the studied indifference with a smile. 'Are you ever going to make a decision?'

Rosanna appeared to think on it for a moment, then smiled shamelessly. 'I don't think so, no.'

Rosanna had been dating two men for the last month. They knew about each other. Hell, they all went clubbing together, the boys' rivalry half jest, half serious. Rosanna, the black widow, liked to have as many in her web as possible to play with. And once they were caught, they were never freed. She had carcasses all over the globe. Emmet and Jay were her latest victims yet somehow she pulled it off with such charm they didn't seem to mind—in fact they salivated over her.

Sophy knew there was a heart of gold underneath the glam. It was just that Rosanna wouldn't admit to it, certainly wouldn't let anyone near it. She spent her life fencing, flirting on a superficial—if somewhat bitchy—plane. Sophy knew why; Rosanna's heart had been broken and she wasn't letting any man near it again. She was only about having light, harmless, fun and keeping any seriousness at a distance.

Sophy's heart had also been broken. Frankly she wanted some of the fun now too—and she knew who with. She walked with Rosanna to the door, waited for the taxi to arrive and tried to absorb some of her friend's zest for life.

Rosanna did all the things Sophy was too 'responsible' to do: she had crazy flings, she went to far flung destinations, she was impulsive and a risk-taker. She did danger—she'd do dangerous like Lorenzo Hall kind of dangerous.

But Sophy had always had more than herself to consider. She loved her parents and had never wanted to embarrass them. As she was the judge's daughter it would have made the perfect salacious storyline—if she'd gone off the rails, been a teen drinker, teen pregnant, or got into drugs. But she'd done none of those things. She'd tried to be the perfect kid—even when she knew she was a disappointment in not following them into the law. She'd even tried to find the perfect boyfriend. If she couldn't live up to the family name she'd marry someone who would. She'd been so naïve—her ex had only wanted her for what he could get out of it—the connection to her family. She supposed it served her right.

She was the boring, goody two-shoes who'd been embarrassingly naïve. Now she was in the habit of playing safe. Not playing at all. Not taking risks.

She never discussed her family with anyone at all now. Privacy had been important anyway, discretion a must. People were put off just as much as they were intrigued, as if they thought she'd run to her father if they mentioned anything even slightly shady. It was as if they expected her to be a pillar of morality, never once veering from doing right.

And in truth she was.

'Is this job full-time?' Rosanna asked.

'Initially.'

'You know your problem, Soph?'

'Go on, enlighten me.'

'You're too sweet. Why don't you ever say no to them? Why don't you ever say no to me?'

'How can I?' Sophy argued. 'You let me move in.' She hadn't wanted to stay with her parents. But hadn't wanted to live alone either—at least, not all the time.

Rosanna shrugged. 'I'm hardly here. It's a selfish move on my part—you're a good house-sitter.'

'Yes.' Sophy laughed, not in the least offended, knowing Rosanna didn't mean it.

'But when are you going to get those pieces finished?'

Sophy bit her lip. She'd known Ro would bring it up eventually. 'I don't know that I can.'

'You're doing it, Sophy. This is such a great opportunity.'

'You've just told me to learn to say no.'

'Only to the things you don't really want. This is something you do want, isn't it? This is something to push for. Put your ambition first for once.'

'I will.' Sophy groaned, but Rosanna was right of course. 'When are you back?'

'Later in the week. Another flying visit home and then off again.'

'You don't get tired of it?'

'No.'

And perhaps if they saw each other more they'd drive each other nuts. The taxi finally pulled up and Rosanna strutted down to get it, her ponytail swinging, her ultra-high heels tapping and her trolley rattling along the concrete path.

'Don't say yes to anything else while I'm away,' she called as she got into the cab. 'I mean it.' She stopped and opened the door again to holler, 'Especially not Lorenzo Hall!'

'Kittens have claws, you know.'

'Not enough to make a mark on a man like him.'

Laughing, Sophy shut the front door. Rested against it for a moment, listening to the vast silence Rosanna had left behind her. She'd been right. Lorenzo was out of her league. And probably not genuinely interested anyway—he was just amusing himself by making her squirm.

Rosanna was right about something else too. Sophy needed to finish up her pieces and prepare for the exhibition. It was a fantastic opportunity and she shouldn't blow it. Inspired, she went into her room and got to work on them—kept working late into the night. Once she got into it the excitement flowed and she decided to make the most of her lunch break—she had no time to waste if she wanted to get enough made.

She got to work early the next day to get ahead. She opened the window in the office to let the fresh spring air in. Looking down, she saw Lorenzo was out the back. Wide brush in hand, he was covering the graffiti with black paint—to match the rest of the fence. So it bothered him enough at last? Sophy thought it was a bit of a shame. But, unable to resist, she watched. His jeans hung that little bit low on his hips, an old tee was stretched across his broad shoulders. His feet were bare. He had his phone trapped between ear and shoulder and his voice carried across the still yard. As did his laughter.

She should probably close the window.

Instead she switched on her computer. She'd concentrate on the work. Not listen to every word winging through the window.

'So what's the castle like?' Lorenzo asked.

Alex had taken Dani to Italy on a belated but extended

honeymoon. They were staying in some castle for a few weeks.

'Amazing. As it should be for the price. How's Cara?'

'Shattered but holding her own, I think.' He swirled the brush through the paint. 'She loved the flowers. She said the baby is tiny but she's doing well.'

'You've not been to see her yet?'

'No.' Lorenzo winced.

'Renz—'

'Not my scene, Alex, you know that.' Happy families weren't him. He was concerned for Cara, of course he was, and he'd sent over a ton of presents, asked if there was anything he could do. Of course there wasn't, she and her husband and their entire extended families had it together. So he didn't have to go and feel awkward around them.

'What about the Whistle Fund? Did you find someone to help out?' Alex moved on.

'Yeah,' Lorenzo sighed. 'Cara did—a friend's younger sister or something. One of those socialites who likes to be involved.' Lorenzo jabbed a fence paling with the brush. 'She's so damn efficient. Organised. Officious. She looks like a frigid girl scout.'

Alex laughed. 'So many adjectives, Renz—she bothering you?'

'No.' If only he knew.

Alex laughed even harder—okay, so he knew he was lying. 'So she's a babe?'

Lorenzo slapped some paint on even thicker. Yes, she was a babe. In more ways than one. All big blue eyes and blonde hair that begged to be ruffled. Hot-looking but with an air of innocence that Lorenzo wasn't at all sure that he should taint. 'She's doing the job. That's all that matters.'

The job would be done—brilliantly—and he'd find a

permanent replacement very soon. Because he had too much else to do to be fixating on her all the time like this.

He ended the call to Alex, finished up the fence. Picking up the can, he swung round, glanced up to the first floor. The window to her office was open but he couldn't see anyone sitting at the desk. Kat must have opened it.

He jogged up to his apartment—scrubbed the paint off in the shower. But he had an itch that just had to be scratched. He had to go have another look, see if he could make her spark again. It was like she'd put some kind of homing device in him, drawing him near. He went down to Reception and stole the mail from Kat's tray. Then his feet just went to where she was.

Irresistible.

'You going out with your boyfriend tonight?' he asked. So lame. So unsubtle.

She froze where she was bent over a pile of papers.

'You should come to the bar. It's the opening night.'

'You're that desperate for customers?' She looked up, all frost. Touchy this morning.

'Actually no. We're confident it'll do the business. I just thought you might like to see it.' He leaned his frame against the door. 'It's a nice little place, intimate. You can cuddle on a sofa in the corner.' Would she be the type to cuddle in public? Somehow he didn't think so—she had that aloof thing going. 'Or you can work up a sweat on the dance floor. Oh…' he paused deliberately '…you'll be on the sofa, then, won't you?'

'I like to dance.'

His muscles tightened at the unexpected tinge of boldness in her tone, he looked harder at her.

'But I already have plans for tonight.' Oh, she was *ultra* cool—it made him suspect she was even hotter beneath.

'With your boyfriend?' Yeah, again, real subtle. But he really needed to know. Now.

Sophy gave up pretending to look at the file in front of her. 'No,' she said as calmly as she could—tricky given the anger zooming round and round her veins, searching for a way out. 'I don't have a boyfriend.'

'No?' Annoyingly he didn't sound that surprised. Worse, he looked pleased about it.

'I don't want one.' Damn, she'd tacked that on too quickly, sounded too vehement. And they both knew it.

His brows lifted. 'Why's that?' He put the mail on her desk, the action bringing him even closer to her. 'Did some twerp break your heart?'

She took a moment to draw breath—so she could answer with icy precision. 'What makes you think I have a heart?' She bit the words out with the experience of seven years' elocution lessons behind her. 'We frigid girl scouts don't bother with them. We find machinery to be more efficient.'

Slowly, deliberately, she lifted her gaze—it clashed with his for a long, long time. His own eyes revealed nothing, yet seemed to penetrate her façade—delving into her secrets. She felt the blush rising—stupidly—when he was the one who'd been so rude. He'd said it. She'd only overheard it by mistake. So why was she the one feeling so uncomfortable now?

'Struck a nerve, did I?' Without breaking the stare he walked around her desk. 'I only said you look like that, not that you actually are.'

'Same difference.' All her nerves were prickling now.

His smile sharpened. 'But I already know you're quite capable of feeling something.'

She just stared at him, fighting to slow her pulse.

'Anger.' He grabbed her arms and pulled her out of the chair. 'Are you very angry with me, Sophy?'

He was inappropriately close—again—holding her tight, yet she didn't fight to step back. She refused to let him intimidate her, or to play with her.

'Do you want me to make it better?' His arms looped around her, hands warm and firm on her waist.

'How are you planning to do that?' She took a quick breath, shaking inside, but stabbed him with some sarcasm. 'With a kiss?'

'Isn't that how it works?' He leaned closer, spearing her with his dark, unreadable eyes. 'Isn't that what you want?'

'No.' Now she was even more angry. Because he was right. It was what she wanted. What she'd been wanting since she first laid eyes on him, and especially since she'd been in his apartment and touched him. But she didn't want it like this. 'I don't think it would make it better.'

'No?'

'I think it would make it worse.' She flashed at him. 'Don't *patronise* me, Lorenzo. You think you're better than me? You think I'm some robot? Some spoilt, bored socialite? Spending all my time doing this and that for everyone else? You think I don't have ambition of my own? Dreams of my own? Desires of my own?'

She shut up, suddenly aware she was verbally vomiting an ancient bitterness that she'd never wanted to talk about to anyone, certainly not to him.

His hold on her tightened. 'I don't think that. But obviously you think some people do.'

Yeah, a little bubbling mass of resentment, that was her.

'Why didn't you say no to working here, if you had other things you wanted to do?' He made it sound so simple.

But she never said no—not to that kind of request. And she did have some time to help. She *liked* to help. It make her feel useful, needed. Except now it felt as if Lorenzo had been laughing at her willingness and her diligence. Were they all laughing at her? Was she valued at all or were her efforts just taken for granted?

Tired. That was her problem. Tired and frustrated and overwhelmed. And he wasn't helping—towering over her like this, tormenting her all the time. She looked straight down to the floor as tears sprang in her eyes. 'Forget it.'

'No.' He took her chin in firm fingers and tilted her head back up so he could see her face. A half-swallowed growl sounded. 'You're really upset.'

'My wounded pride will get over it,' she snapped, cross with her stupid weakness. 'I don't care what you think. I'm here to do a job. Now I'm going to get on with it.'

'Not until I apologise.'

'I didn't think you'd be the type to say sorry.'

'And you think I'm the one making assumptions?' His eyes glinted but the smallest of smiles appeared. 'Okay, I don't say it often. But when I do, I mean it.' He stroked her jaw. 'I'm sorry.'

'It's fine.' She shrugged, too crushed to accept it with good grace and determined not to let that smile have its usual disabling effect. 'I don't care what you think about me.'

His smile deepened just a touch. Okay, so she was protesting too much.

She sighed as a flicker of good humour returned to her. 'Don't get big-headed about it. I care too much what everyone thinks about me.'

'What you think matters to me too.'

Okay, so now his niceness was making it worse. Embarrassed, she shifted. 'Look, just forget it.'

'No.' His grip tightened. 'I'm going to make it better. I'm going to do it anyway. It's been on the cards for days. You know that.'

She froze, her body rendered immobile with anticipation overload. All she could do was gaze up at him—drowning in his eyes, yearning for that beautiful mouth to touch her.

And then it did.

A butterfly-light brush of lips on skin—a shade too close to her mouth to be a safe kiss on the cheek. And he lingered too long for it to be safe too.

'Better?' His question almost inaudible, but she heard it, *felt* it as his lips grazed her as he asked.

'No.'

The smallest of pauses as they stood—intent hovering. Only a couple of inches separated their bodies, only a millimetre separated their lips. She could feel his heat, and smell his fresh soapy scent. A tremor ran through her as anticipation almost broke her nerve. Suddenly he moved—that merest fraction, the littlest drop to her mouth. His lips were warm, and they clung.

Her eyes closed, her body blanking everything so it could focus only on the touch. His gentleness so unexpected, the rush of sensation pierced through her.

A moan—was it her? The softness, the slowness, the sweetness overwhelmed her. She trembled again and his hands tightened. This wasn't enough.

And then it was over.

She couldn't breathe. She saw his eyes zooming in on her. Jet black now. Intense. Beautiful. Time and motion stopped for a moment that felt like infinity. Her every nerve was wired, waiting, wanting. Would he come back—would he kiss her again?

'No,' he said roughly, stepping back. His hands dropped—leaving her suddenly cold. 'You were right. I was wrong.' He walked out of the door. 'I really am sorry.'

CHAPTER FOUR

SOPHY managed to stay standing 'til Lorenzo was out of sight, then collapsed into the chair. Fisting her hands over her eyes, shoulders rising—blocking all sensation. Just for a second. Just to stay sane. Her whole body tingled, as if she'd been zapped by some kind of extra-terrestrial ray-gun making all her cells jiggle.

The disappointment was devastating.

Why had he stopped? She *knew* he'd felt it—she'd seen it in his eyes, heard it in his voice. But he'd practically run away.

If she was Rosanna she'd have been the one to move that second time. It would have taken nothing—the slightest tilt of her chin to resume the contact. She'd had it on a platter. Yet she hadn't taken the chance.

Now she was mad with herself for wishing she had, even madder for having been so damn passive. Why hadn't she had the guts to take the risk? But she'd been knocked—first by his words, second by the kiss and the emotion that had flooded through her.

And now he was sorry? Not just for what she'd over-heard, but for kissing her. She understood. But she couldn't understand how he could regret it. He'd felt it as she had; that kind of chemistry couldn't be one-sided.

And she wanted more. She *really* wanted more. A fire

had been lit in her belly and it needed feeding. Except it looked as if she was going to be left starving.

Well, she was taking her lunch break today. She was working to rule and jolly well going to work on her own project. Spurred on by what she'd said to him—she *did* have her own ambition. And now, more than ever, she was determined to make it. She'd do this exhibition and show them all she had more to her than great organisational skills. She had dreams—and she'd make them real.

That had been a mistake. Oh, man, had that been a mistake. Lorenzo's body hurt as he moved—every cell rebelling as he made himself walk away.

Yeah, she had emotions all right—her want for him so hot and sweet. He wanted to bury himself completely in the delectable softness she offered.

She'd stared at him. Just waiting with her eyes so huge. It was like corrupting an innocent. She really was a good girl, wasn't she? And Lorenzo never messed with good girls. Ever. Things got too messy. And it was obvious things with Sophy would get nuclear messy. Hell, she'd been crushed by that stupid comment he'd made to Alex. Her big eyes brimming with hurt—from just a few silly words. And he felt bad for it—an absolute heel. Because she hadn't deserved it. He didn't like feeling guilty.

And now he knew for sure there was no way in hell she was frigid. She wasn't just warm either. She had volcanic qualities. Like a snow-capped mountain, she was capable of blasting fire when you least expected it, able to melt granite with her heat.

That just made it fifty times worse because he *ached* to make her tremble again and again. Being with her, in her, would be more than explosive, it would be some kind of divine experience. But if she was hurt by just a few words, no way could she handle a short-term fling. And that was all he ever did. She was a relationship woman. Ms Monogamous.

She was far too good for him—literally. He just wasn't crossing that line. It didn't matter how hot he was for her, it wasn't going to happen. Because Mr Monogamous he wasn't. He'd tried it once when he'd been young and naïve enough to think the past wouldn't matter. He'd been shot down and wasn't taking a hit like that again. Sure, he liked women—lots of women—for the physical fun of sex. No more than three times with a partner—preferably in the same night. That wasn't a kind of deal straight, sweet Sophy could handle.

But he couldn't stay away, not all day. He told himself he couldn't be rude and ignore her after what had happened. Somehow he had to get them back to a purely professional footing. Going to be tricky given he was the one who'd been flashing skin the whole time.

She was at the desk, her head bent as she concentrated on the stuff in front of her—piles of tiny objects. She had a bag open on the edge of the desk, small sharp-looking tools to one side while she made her decisions. It was the first time he'd seen her actually sitting still and not busily typing while filing and talking to someone on the phone all at the same time. Now she was so concentrated, so quiet, looking so intently at the stuff on the table in front of her. He leaned his shoulder against the door jamb and said nothing. Just waited for her to realise he was there, enjoying the time he had to observe.

It was several minutes until she glanced up, did a double take and squeaked.

'Oh, sorry.' The tempting colour rose under her skin. 'I didn't hear you.'

'What are you doing?' He'd figured it out already but

didn't want to admit just how long he'd been standing watching her like some stalker.

Her hands moved, as if to hide it from him, her serenity broken as she started packing it all away. A velvet covered board with grooves in it into which she was arranging small semi-precious stones or beads or other bits.

'It's okay,' he said, wishing he hadn't shattered her moment of calm so completely. It was as if he'd tripped the switch and now the efficient automaton was back. 'You're allowed a lunch break.' Except lunch had been hours ago. Had the goody two-shoes abandoned her job all afternoon?

She looked guilty.

Yep, he'd caught her out. He couldn't stop his mile wide smile. 'What are you making?'

She blinked at him, hurriedly looked away. 'A necklace.'

'A hobby of yours?' He saw her tension spike.

Then she nodded. All back to brisk. 'Yes.'

He watched as the guilt gave her an all-over-body sweep of red.

'Sorry,' she muttered. 'I lost track of time.'

She was just never going to be a cheat, was she? Never going to be someone who could do something she shouldn't and not own up about it. He bet she'd never done anything remotely dodgy in her whole life. Jeez, they were poles apart.

'Don't worry about it.' He didn't care. She'd done an amazing job clearing up the mess that was the Whistle Fund office. Everything was running on schedule again. Even the opening of the bar looked as if it was going to go off okay. The chaos of the last couple of weeks seemed to be at an end. In no small part thanks to Sophy. She was allowed an afternoon to slack off. 'Just go home early. You've done heaps already.'

She lifted her head, the cool look back. 'Okay. Thanks.'

He lingered for a half second too long, tempted to say or do something more. Finally he made himself turn and walk along to his own office. It had just been a kiss. Nothing more than that. He could forget it. He could ignore the tantalising prospect of seducing her. Sure he could.

At least try to do the right thing, Lorenzo—for once in your life.

Sophy hadn't had any sleep. She'd sat up late again, working on her pieces. Unhappy with the necklace she'd made the night before. Her jewellery had to be something really special—couldn't be something anyone could make in their own home if they had the time and the inclination. It was all about the eye, the detail and the little spark of difference. She had the resources—had been collecting vintage bits and bobs for years. Had gathered a lot while in Europe and had got invaluable experience when she'd worked on the floor of a jewellery shop in France. She'd spent her lunch breaks sitting in the workshop with the jewellers learning some of the finer points. She'd done a few courses too, so she had a reasonably solid technique now. But she didn't have so much time to make the amount she needed for the show. And she wasn't sure she had them exactly how she wanted them.

But on top of everything she was distracted. Wished Rosanna were on hand to help her out—with Vamp 101 classes.

She didn't see Lorenzo all morning. But early afternoon, as the sun was hitting its zenith, she heard that familiar sound. She looked out of the open window. He was on his makeshift basketball court, wearing jeans of course. But his torso was covered this time—with a loose NBA style singlet.

He glanced up to the window, saw she was watching. She pulled her head back in but she saw his grin. He bounced the ball a few times. Executed some fancy run up to the board and jumped high—landing the shot.

He glanced back up to her. Yeah, okay, she was still watching and he knew it. Too slowly he lifted the hem of his singlet, used it to wipe the sweat from his brow—revealing his abs in the process. Deliberately. Provocatively.

He lifted his head and looked up at her. He wanted a reaction? Impossible—she couldn't move, just stared at him.

His smile appeared and both his hands moved to the hem of his singlet. In a flash he'd whipped it over his head—tossing it to the side.

Oh God, she just couldn't take it any more. She slammed her window shut. Heard his laugh anyway. That tore it. She stood and marched downstairs, opened the back door, let it slam behind her. He turned, she saw his surprise. So he was just winding her up? He'd pay.

She walked past him and went to where the ball was rolling towards the fence, scooped it up. It was bigger than the netball she used to play with. She prayed to the sporting gods for some kind of benevolence. It had been years since she last played netball, but she had been Goal Attack—responsible for shooting through the hoops. She rolled the ball against her palms, pulling it in tight to her chest, getting the feel for it. She was too steamed to care much anyway. Really she felt like throwing the thing at his head rather than the hoop.

She turned. He was too close behind her. She gave him a pointed look and he took a step to the side. Neither said anything. She looked up at the basket. So damn high. Still, she had energy in her muscles that needed to be expended.

She aimed and threw. The net swished as the ball slid through. Confidence from her success swamped her and she turned to stare hotly at him.

'Been keeping secrets?' His voice was low. 'You want to play with me, Sophy?'

'I want to beat you.'

His whole body tensed. She saw the electricity surge in him.

'No one beats me.'

'Not afraid, are you, Lorenzo?'

The briefest pause and then that smile curled. 'What are we playing for?' He quietly walked closer.

Yeah, she'd hoped she could bring out his wicked side. She just hadn't realised quite how easy it would be. 'What do you want to play for?'

Was this her? Leaning provocatively close to him, practically purring?

His amusement deepened but it didn't bother her, for she saw the fire too. 'You're the one suggesting the game; you come up with the prize.'

She just stared at him, letting her eyes say it all.

'Really?' He dropped the basketball. It rolled away, coming to a rest against the newly painted fence.

'Don't you think?'

He'd gone very still. 'I'm not sure either of us is thinking.'

'Isn't it going to happen anyway? Hasn't it been on the cards for days?' She angled her head and studied him, half dying inside now with her boldness. He was so silent. Too silent. 'Do you really want to stop it?'

His hands were on his hips, his biceps flexing. 'We probably should.'

'Why?' She could see his chest rising and falling faster than before. She knew he felt it too.

Angry fingers suddenly gripped her upper arms. 'Why are you chasing this?'

She flinched. Chasing? Like some infatuated teen stalking her first prey? Shocked, she blurted the truth. 'I've never done this before. I've never had a fling. Never had a one night stand. I've always been "good", always watched out for my reputation, always gone out with "safe" guys.' She'd had a couple of steady boyfriends, then that engagement. She shut her mind to the memory, turned back to the heat of the moment. 'Just for once I want the freedom to do what I want to do, take what I want, have what I want.'

'And *I'm* what you want?' His jaw was rigid, the strength in his fingers not easing an iota.

She glanced down his body. 'You're very fit.'

'What is it that's really turning you on? Going with someone outside your select social circle? Someone from the wrong side of the tracks, someone rougher? Is that what I am to you?'

Her senses flared at the word rougher. She could do with some rough right now. 'I don't care about your background.' She didn't actually care about *him*—did she? 'Like I said, you're just very fit.' She sighed, frustrated. 'And every time I see you, you're half naked. What do you expect? I'm only human.'

A short laugh was shaken from him. 'So you just want physical, Sophy?'

'Really physical.'

The breath whistled out between his teeth. She held her breath, frozen as she watched him decide.

'I don't do relationships, Sophy.'

'You think I don't know that?'

His fingers relaxed but didn't let her go and his smile returned. 'This is not going to get out of hand.'

She stepped closer, anticipation twisting with satisfaction and spiralling higher. She'd won. For once she'd been bold and it had worked. 'Of course not. You're going to be very much in hand.' She smiled. Really, dirty flirty talk was easy. She could so be the queen of it here.

'I think you're confused about who's going to be dominant.' His hands tightened again, drawing her closer still. 'I'll be in control, Sophy—you don't want to be.'

That was exactly it. She didn't want to be in control any more. She just wanted to feel. Not think. Just experience it, release the tension from her system. 'Okay.'

His expression flared. His hands moved, looping round her back, imprisoning her. 'So what did you have in mind?'

'What about my office?'

'*Now?*' He laughed freely. 'A late afternoon lay? Just before you leave?'

'It has a certain appeal.' Her eyelids were heavy, her cheeks flushed. She'd wanted him for days, of course she wanted him now.

'Aren't you getting ahead of yourself?' His voice dropped to a carnal whisper, but his eyes were like polished stones. 'We've barely kissed. We might not be that good.'

Barely kissed? Oh, he was full of it. Her lips curved into a lush, lazy smile. 'You don't believe that. Besides...' she skated the tips of her fingers over his jaw, shivering with the pleasure of being able to touch '...you do everything to a brilliant standard.'

'So do you.'

Not quite true, but she was happy to skip it. 'Then we'll

be brilliant together, won't we?' She was wholly leaning against him now, feeling the heat of him through her linen shirt. 'Let's try it out.'

'Oh, Sophy,' he muttered, his face even more angular. 'You'd better know what you're doing.'

In answer she lifted her face, inviting it all.

In a fast movement he caught her mouth with his. It wasn't anything like the gentle kiss of the day before. This was brazenly sexual—branding her with its heat. She gasped, held back for a scrap of a second beneath the bruising, blazing invasion. Then threw herself headlong into the eye of the storm, locking her hands behind his neck, letting her breasts press against him. His hands pushed her tighter against his hardness. And he was hard all over.

His heated skin melted her. His tongue swept between her lips, she parted to let him in as deep as he wanted. Twirled her tongue around his and felt his grip tighten even harder on her.

Yes.

Her neck muscles strained as she pushed up into his kiss, not wanting the searing assault to ease even a smidge. She rocked her hips. Rising onto tiptoe to feel that bulging ridge nearer to where she really wanted it, rubbed closer again, desperate to relieve the agony that now flared deep within. She felt rather than heard his grunt. His hand cupped her butt, fingers firm on her flesh, holding her as he rocked back against her—his thrusting slow, devastating, while his mouth was still sealed to hers. His tongue teased into her the way she really wanted that other part of him to. Her moan reverberated between them then. Oh, yes. That was what she wanted. All the strength of him ripping into her.

His kiss altered, breaking but quickly returning. Nipping at her mouth he pushed her harder against his straining erection. She shifted her feet to part her legs that fraction more, rotating the half centimetre she could against him, torturing them both. She cursed the clothes that were scrunching between them. He bent her back to force her body closer still, until all she could do was cling to his shoulders and accept his demands. She didn't want to stand any more anyway. She wanted to lie down. She wanted him to pin her with his weight and pound into her. Fast, hard, now.

All her desire unleashed with just the one kiss.

He took the weight of one breast in his hand and her body buckled with the sensation. 'Yes.' Her high cry, half whispered.

So there was such a thing as pure, carnal lust. An attraction to a body, where nothing else mattered but touching it, feeling it and making its beauty come alive. There could be a free, physical joy. She'd been missing out for years—had always taken everything too seriously, been too cautious. She swept her hand hard across his shoulder, up his neck and into his hair, clutching to his deliciously dangerous heat. It was time to play catch-up.

Lorenzo fought hard with his raging lust, and hers, easing them out of the kiss, forcing his hands to slow and then to stop their exploration of her skin. It hurt.

He lifted his mouth a millimetre away from hers. Saw that passion had made her blue eyes glow more vividly than ever before. He couldn't resist another brushing kiss, nor could he resist the way her nipple was pressing into his palm. His fingers mirrored the action of his mouth—brushing the sensitive nub just as his lips did hers.

Very, very lightly.

Her shudder nearly had him on his knees. He'd wanted to test her—to see if she really meant it. So he'd kissed her hard. No gentle beginning, no tenderness, just the brunt of his raw, blistering passion.

And she'd met him, matched him. Almost *beaten* him.

Now he wanted to strip her, to kiss her, to make the whole of her wet with want. He wanted her drenched with desire—and him too—for their bodies to slide together, fighting for that furious, physical release. He hadn't wanted sex so badly in ages.

Instead he pushed away, made himself take a whole step. Forced his feet to move another. 'I'm not going to take you now,' he said breathlessly. Telling himself as much as her. 'Not like this.'

'Why not?' She didn't seem to realise the extent to which she was giving herself away.

His body tightened, the animal part of him so keen to take up her unguarded offer. To topple her here and now and be done with it. But he couldn't. She needed some breathing space to be sure. He needed her to be sure. The lust was hot enough to make them both brainless. Do something she yet might regret. Lorenzo couldn't bear those regrets—not his, not hers either.

Stupid. Since when did he care? Since when did he let any kind of second thoughts stop him from having a good time?

Because she'd told him—she didn't usually do this. He'd known that already but having her actually say it made it worse. She needed to be certain. He didn't want any uncomfortable ramifications. 'Are you sure you can handle it?'

She turned away. He saw the chill descend, the stiffening in her shoulders. 'Don't treat me like an idiot. Of course I can. We're only talking one night, Lorenzo.'

He ruffled his hair, needing to get his conflicting emotions under control. Hell, it was one p.m. and he was this close to having her in a quickie session at the back of the

warehouse. He wanted more than a quickie. He wanted a
bed. He wanted the whole night.

One night—her suggestion.

His body chafed—eager to take the offer up now. But no
way was he taking her upstairs to his apartment. Inviting
her in there might lead to mixed messages. He'd have to
take her out. Damn, a date meant more too—or might to
her. He shook his head, could she really keep it uncomplicated? But he wanted it too much to say no. The burning need forced him to take the risk. 'I'll take you out
tonight.'

'That's not necessary.'

Oh, she was cool, wasn't she? His edgy feeling sharpened. Had he underestimated her entirely? 'You don't want
to go out?'

She looked evasive. 'You could come over to my
place.'

It was probably a good idea. He didn't like that it had
come from her, but she was right. Better not for them to go
out together—looking like lovers, feeling like lovers. But
ironically nor did he want some sordid assignation. Just
for him to knock on the door and her let him in—literally.
The warring feelings frustrated him. 'For dinner?'

'If you like,' she answered carelessly, giving him an
address, a time.

He stared at her as she spoke, tried to figure out what
the hell she was thinking. Failed. But she'd come to him.
She was asking him. If she wanted to go through with it,
who was he to say no? He'd never been one to turn down
an opportunity. 'Okay.'

She smiled, and walked back inside.

He glanced up to the window and waited. Soon saw her
swinging into her role as the perfect administrator again. It
should please him, not annoy him—given she was on the

payroll and all. But for some reason he found it incredibly irritating. She could go back and concentrate on boring work just like that?

Man, he wanted to see her out of control. He wanted the perfect clothes crushed and the never-out-of-place hair messy. He wanted her eyes wide and wild and her mouth parted as she panted. He wanted her both laughing and crying with pleasure so intense that she was no longer in charge of anything. He wanted her to writhe for him.

And he wanted it now.

CHAPTER FIVE

LORENZO had been fantasising about this for too long. That was why he was so edgy. Had Sophy known the XXX rating of his dreams, she'd never have offered him this kind of access. The things he wanted to do...

He took a deep breath. Her home was as he'd expected. A cute little villa in the heart of poshville. Just the place for a young Auckland socialite. He walked up the path with the fatalistic feeling growing inside him. He hadn't brought flowers, not even a bottle of wine. Just himself. His body was what she wanted—and it was all she was getting. He shook off the clanging bell of doom—stupid. This was just going to be some hot sex—nothing more.

She answered the door swiftly. Delicate colour sat high in her cheeks. She'd changed her clothes. Wearing a different blouse, a casual skirt that flared out, emphasising her little waist. Sandals on her feet. Pink polish gleaming on her toenails. Her hair was styled in that nineteen-fifties Hollywood-starlet style.

'I didn't cook. Sorry. Been busy.'

Getting ready for him? He liked that idea a little too much.

She turned and led him down the polished wooden hallway.

'It's okay.' He wasn't that hungry anyway. Not for food.

'I cheated and picked up some stuff from the deli.' She led him to the dining area. 'Thought we could snack.'

'Sure.' He looked at the table. She'd unloaded the deli pots into pretty little dishes. Floral. Heaven help him. Fragile fine bone china. That was her all over.

She was watching him, a knowing look in her eyes that unsettled him more. 'You're not having regrets already?'

'I don't do regrets. Why, do you?'

She shook her head. 'New Year's resolution not to.'

Yeah, right. 'You've never done anything to regret, have you?' He couldn't hold back the bitter note of accusation.

'You think?' She stepped up to him. 'I'm no angel, Lorenzo.' She leaned forward and whispered, 'And I'm no virgin. You're not going to hurt me.'

He swallowed. For someone who'd said she'd never done this before, she was holding her own. So the snacking could wait a while. There was something far more pressing to be done. He lifted a hand and stroked her hair, gathered a lock and ran his finger and thumb along the length of it. He tugged gently, straightening the curl at the bottom. When he let it go it bounced right back. 'So you're sure.'

A look of irritation crossed her face. 'You know I am. You're here, I'm here. End of conversation.'

He laughed inwardly. It seemed he wasn't the only one to have been dreaming of this for too long. He watched her, waited and soon saw the slight nervousness steal into her eyes, despite her words. She'd taken a smidge of her lower lip between her teeth, he could see her biting hard on it. And she was staying very, very still—waiting.

He leaned forward and so slowly, so gently caught that lower lip between his own teeth. She gasped, freeing it so it was his. He sucked on it, let his tongue run over the swell of soft flesh. She opened for him completely—and they hurtled straight back into the red-hot kiss of earlier.

Her hands lifted to his shoulders; he liked the feel of them, he liked the feel of her hips digging into him too. It was as if everywhere they touched the power surged, pulsing between them.

He broke free, determined to slow it down. 'You don't want to eat first?'

'Can't you just shut up and get on with it?' She thrust against him again. 'Anyone would think you're stalling.'

He looked at the gleam in her eyes. The nerves had gone. She was enjoying being provocative now. And she wanted it fast. Too bad. She'd told him the truth earlier. She wasn't a one-night-only girl. Not before now.

'What's wrong?' he asked bluntly. 'Why do you want it to be over so quick?' Did she want it done and then him leave inside the hour? Like some naughty fantasy that she could tell herself wasn't really real?

Not happening. If she wanted it, then she was getting it—one *whole* night. And one night didn't mean once only. And it certainly didn't mean quick.

She didn't answer, had fallen silent, breathless as she leaned her lower belly against him. He understood—even just that simple closeness turned him on too. He traced her collarbones with the tips of his fingers. Watched for the reaction. Yeah, there it was. The widening of her pupils and the increase in her breathing. Her response so quick, so gorgeous. Impulsively he leaned forward and kissed her cheek.

She turned her head but he didn't take the mouth she offered. Instead he kissed her ear, let his tongue lightly trace the whorls, let his teeth gently bite on the soft lobe.

Then he kissed the skin just below—she shivered. Yes, she was sensitive there, vulnerable.

He liked to touch her where she was vulnerable.

The constraint fell from him. Too late to pull back

now. Inside he knew it had always been too late—from the moment he'd seen her looking so crossly at him at the back of the warehouse he'd wanted her. And he was going to get what he wanted—now.

She moved restlessly. He saw the flicker in her eyes but he refused to kiss her again. Not yet—he needed to regain his control so he could play with her the way he wanted. He undid each button on her blouse, so slowly, until it fell open. He pushed it back on her shoulders, took in the pretty bra. White, floral lace. Very pretty—but the soft globes it encased were even prettier. He could see her lush nipples pressing against the lace and nearly groaned aloud.

He had to kiss her again, not her mouth—not yet—but the soft creamy column of her throat. He brushed his lips against it, felt her pulse beating beneath him, breathed in the subtle scent that he found so sexy. Her head fell back, giving him greater access to that sensitive area. He traversed down, seeking to anoint more of the sweet skin with his tongue, his lips, eventually crossing over her collarbones and to the rising slope of her breasts.

Her hands lifted to his waist, pulling on the belt loops of his jeans, trying to draw him closer. He refused to move. So she did. Rising to tiptoe, bumping against him. He smiled as he hit the lace edging of her bra.

'Lorenzo.' The need made her voice sound raw.

He slid his hands up her thighs, soothing the ache he knew she was feeling with the promise of that intimate caress. Soon. Very soon. He was so glad she was wearing a skirt.

'Lorenzo, please.' She swirled harder against him.

He felt her hands on his back, on his skin as she went beneath his tee shirt. He tensed. He couldn't handle her touch just yet. He lifted his fingers higher against her, swept them across the front of her panties.

She jumped. Stepped back from him.

He froze.

She wasn't looking at him. 'Like the good little girl scout I am, I'm prepared,' she gabbled, fumbling with her skirt. He watched narrow-eyed. Finally she pulled a condom out of her pocket with shaking fingers. But she dropped it as soon as she had it. She groaned with frustration.

He spared a quick glance down to where it had fallen and then stepped forward and slid his hand round the back of her neck, pulling her to him. 'We don't need it.' He bent and resumed his savouring of her skin.

'We don't?' She sounded startled.

He bit back the laugh—barely succeeded. 'Not yet.'

'No?' She was panting now, her hips circling again, pushing into his in that way that was slowly driving him out of his mind.

He gripped her butt, stopped her. 'No. Not yet.'

He was determined to have his slow discovery of her, but he'd give her a taste of what was to come. He kissed his way across her breast, moving up the gentle slope, finally taking the nub deep into his mouth, his tongue raking over the tip—pretty lace and all.

She cried out. He felt the satisfaction burning into him. Couldn't resist sucking harder, letting her feel the edge of his teeth. She jerked, and he clutched her closer, stopping her from slipping to the floor.

Her hands clasped his shoulders. He lifted away from her so he could see into her eyes and tease the hell out of her. 'You're not that well prepared, are you?'

Looking dazed, confused, she said nothing.

'Don't you think we might need more than one?' He straightened and set her right on her feet again, dug one hand into his back pocket and pulled out the stash he'd stuffed in there earlier. Holding his hand in front of her, he uncurled his fingers and half a dozen condoms scattered on the floor between them.

He caught her round the waist as he felt her soften. 'Now stop trying to control me.' He pushed her into the dining chair, and went down in front of her. Placed his palms on the inside of her knees and pushed them apart.

'What are you doing?'

'Maximising pleasure,' he muttered, hands sliding up her thighs. 'It's like making wine, Sophy—producing the best takes time. Patience. A gentle touch.'

'But I like to get things done.'

'I know you do. And this is one thing we're going to do very thoroughly.' He slid his hands back down to her knees, skimmed them down to her ankles.

This wasn't going to be quick. He'd wanted too long. He was going to touch every sweet part of her—and make her mindless.

Sophy looked down as he knelt between her legs. His eyes jet black, his face concentrated as he watched his fingers trace over her soft skin. He bent and she closed her eyes. Yes. There it was. That sensual mouth, those full lips brushing against her—setting every tiny spot he touched on fire. Someone had to help her—*he* did. She just couldn't take this kind of torture.

'Lorenzo.' But there was no point—he wasn't in any hurry as he kissed across her thighs. She tilted her hips towards him in an ancient rhythm, mentally begging him to go higher, to where she needed him. Finally his hands glided to her hips, his fingers grasping the elastic. She pressed her heels into the floor, lifted her butt from the chair so he could slide her knickers down. In seconds his hands were back at her knees, pushing them wide again. She screwed her eyes shut tighter.

But the kiss she expected didn't come. It was her breasts

that he touched, nuzzling through the lace, his hands pushing her skirt up higher around her waist.

She could feel the heat of his torso so close, she wanted it closer. She honestly thought she was going to die, she wanted him so badly. 'Please, Lorenzo. Please.'

'No.' His half-laugh was unbearably wicked.

'I can't wait any longer.' The touch of his lips to her nipples sent an SOS to her cervix—starting the contractions, the searing need of her sex to have his.

'Yes, you can.'

'But if I come now, I won't…' How could she make him understand? She didn't want the edge taken off her hunger, she wanted all of him inside her when she had the release. She wanted it to be the best she'd ever had—she could almost taste it. 'I want it *all*.' All at once. Immediately. She was reduced to basic instinct now—to demand his possession.

He laughed. 'You'll have me. Again and again. I promise. Why not just enjoy this moment?'

She was going to go insane, that was why. The volcano inside her threatened to erupt. He moved—but not how she'd wanted—not to pull her to the floor so he could thrust into her in the way she was so desperate for.

No. It was only a slight change in hold but it was enough to bring her firmly under his control. He spread one hand wide on the inside of her thigh, placed his other much higher, cupping her breast, his fingers caressing her painfully taut nipple. But she could no longer move, her body bound by his, utterly enthralled by the simplest of touches: he licked her.

She gasped as his tongue swirled, tasting, teasing her most intimate, most sensitive part.

And it killed her.

She pushed back against the hard chair, unashamedly

thrusting her pelvis into him. The waves of pleasure lapping at her, as he lapped her. Oh he knew what to do, how she wanted him to do it. The waves rose higher, starting to wash over her—every muscle tensed, tingled.

'Don't stop, please don't stop,' she begged him, shaking as she felt it surging. She wanted it, but she wanted more. She didn't know what to do with her hands, with her heart, with the heat burning her inside out. In the end she reached out and drove them into his hair. Thick and vibrant beneath her fingertips, the texture rough and all male. Her head hit the back of the chair as she arched higher to meet his kiss—tension locking her body in an endless moment of stillness. His hand went from her thigh to support her beneath—holding her to his hungry mouth so he could go deeper, suck and stroke harder. And he didn't stop. The slow, rhythmic, divine touches intensified. Her fingers curled into claws as she shook, her cry high and harsh. And as she buckled he still didn't stop, not giving her any respite, forcing every last ripple of response from her—until neither her body nor mind could take any more and the world went black.

Sophy was no longer a sentient being. She couldn't think, couldn't move, couldn't speak. Couldn't even open her eyes. His hands traced over her. Gentle kisses followed their path. It was as if he was worshipping her skin, her scent, her sex.

Her pulse slowed, steadied and then started to leisurely rise again as she heard him murmuring her name. She opened her eyes then. He lifted his head from her skin, met her gaze, his smile almost boyish with pleasure. He knew, he knew just how well he'd thrilled her and how ready she was for him to do it again. Like now.

'You still want it all?'

'More than ever,' she answered honestly.

His smile faded as his hand cupped her jaw. 'You humble me.'

He twisted away, grabbed a few of the condoms. Once on his feet he lifted her into his arms and walked, instinctively stopping at the door to the master bedroom.

'Not that one.' She was in the smaller of the two rooms.

He placed her in the middle of her bed. Stood back and whipped his tee shirt from his head. 'I think you'd better take off your bra and skirt.'

She was too busy enjoying watching him strip to bother with that. He took a moment with his jeans, taking care with the zip.

When finally, jaw-droppingly naked, he ripped open a little pack and rolled the condom over his erection, his teeth clenched for the few seconds it took.

Then he looked up at her. Frowned. 'Bra and skirt Sophy? I'll lose it if I do it.'

Maybe she wanted him to lose it.

'If you want me inside you then you have to do it.'

She smiled, thrilled to see him so tense. But she knelt up on the bed and twisted her arms behind her back to undo her bra clasp.

He stood at the foot of her bed, looking like some ancient Greek athlete—no, some ancient Greek *god*.

And the look on his face made her feel like a goddess. She stood on the bed then, unzipped her skirt, and with a shimmy of her hips let it fall.

He stood stiller than a statue.

Legs apart, she put her hands on her hips, filled with a new confidence—just from the way he was watching her. 'What are you waiting for?'

He answered slowly, through clenched teeth. 'Some degree of control.'

She dropped to her knees and crawled to the end of the bed. Straightened up and put her hand on his chest—watching it rise and fall. Then she looked up into his searing black gaze.

His fingers tangled in her hair, twisting in her curls, and he pulled. She didn't resist, let her head fall back so her mouth was his to plunder. And he did.

But then she ran both hands through his hair, holding him to her as she let herself fall back onto the mattress. As she intended, he overbalanced and came down hard on top of her.

'Sophy,' he grunted, automatically bracing a hand on either side of her, lifting his weight off her. 'You okay?'

She hooked her legs around him, arched up to stop him moving too far away. 'No. I'm tired of waiting for you.'

'I can't wait any more.'

She smiled and rippled beneath him. 'Good.'

He stayed braced above her for a long moment, gazing into her eyes. She lifted her hips, trying to hurry him. He just smiled—that heart-meltingly brilliant smile. Then he lowered his weight half onto her again. Her heartbeat rocketed. Anticipation made breathing difficult. At last he moved, a smooth powerful stroke forward, filling her in the one hit.

She gasped, expelled an even harsher breath as she shook.

'You okay?' He moved again.

'Yes,' she panted. 'Yes. Yes. Yes.' But her breathing pitched wildly, the blackness threatening again as she gasped, struggling to cope with the blissful sensations. Too much, it was too much.

'Easy honey.' He pressed into her once more—slow,

deliberate—and held there until she steadied. The weight of him and his careful hold anchored her, but his power had the potential to pull her apart. After a wavering moment, she began to breathe more deeply, softening, increasingly able to handle the intensity.

He kissed her, a soothing kiss. 'Stay with me,' he muttered.

She nodded, feeling his slow rhythm begin again, and she started to move with him this time. She ran her hands over his back, feeling the strength he had to offer her. She smiled as she felt it surge beneath her fingers. In her most secret fantasies she'd never imagined it would be like this.

'Yeah.' He kissed her properly then.

She took his face in her hands and kissed him back—as deeply as she possibly could. As the feelings ratcheted she felt him grow more tense. Until he wrenched his mouth from hers and bored a burning look into her, the smile gone, *his* breathing ragged and uneven now.

He rose higher above her, working them both harder, until she started to lose it again. Then he kissed her jaw, her ears, her brow, her neck, while his hips moved in that maddening, magical way. All at once the sensations rushed at her from every direction. She was half panting, half crying, mostly screaming. And just like that, too soon, not soon enough, she shattered. Her body convulsed in ecstasy, clamping hard—forcing utter capitulation from him too.

The tips of his fingers touched her damp skin. 'So you do sweat.'

'Contrary to popular opinion, I am actually human,' she answered with her eyes closed.

'And do you like it when I make you sweat?'

She didn't answer. He'd had enough from her already. He'd had everything.

'Your hair is still perfect.' He ran his fingers through it. 'What do you do to it?'

She made herself answer this time—keep the conversation on this light level. Even though she felt as if she were on shakier ground than if she were standing on the rim of an active volcano. Really she didn't want to talk at all. She just wanted to absorb herself again. Right now she felt all that was precious in her was hanging up in the air, able to be seen—and shot down. She wanted to suck it back up. 'Nothing. It's just the way it is.' She knew he didn't believe her. But it was true—she could only have the one style. Boring as anything.

'I don't think I've ever seen you so still.'

She turned her head and looked at him. 'What do you mean?'

He lay on his side, facing her, watching her with an impudent grin. 'You're usually doing a million things, ever so efficiently, never stopping.'

'I only work fast because I want to get the job done. There are other things I want to be doing.'

He levered up higher on his arm, glanced around her room. At the table. 'Making the necklaces?'

She was such an open book, wasn't she? 'Yes. And other pieces.' She watched him closely. If he dared laugh she'd brain him one. She'd hidden it from her parents. Her brother and sister had teased her one too many times about never getting over the toddler threading beads phase. She was just the child who'd been unable to live up to their achievements, was only useful as the errand girl.

And the silly thing was she *was* like a child—eager for their acceptance. But she couldn't help that craving. She'd never been one to disrespect her parents, always had been dutiful. But she wanted more than that; she wanted to make them proud. She wanted them to value her contribution to the world as much as they valued her brother and sister's and their own. Trouble was, she was hardly off saving people as they were.

He'd hopped off the bed and was looking at the pieces on the desk. 'They're pretty good.'

'And you're an expert?'

He whirled, looked all wolf. 'I've seen a few necklaces in my time.'

Of course he had. He'd seen a few necks, hadn't he? And he knew how to make love to a woman's neck, that was for sure. The niggle she felt about that was shamefully fleeting. She just wanted him to do it again.

He looked at the tray of beads and glass and trinkets. 'They're different.'

'Thank you.'

'You've got a few done.'

Sophy hesitated. Then the small burst of pride beat over her usual reticence. She wanted to impress him—just a little. 'I'm putting them in a show.'

As soon as she'd said it she regretted it. The nerves flared—what if no one liked them? What if she sold none?

'What show?'

'There's a film festival coming up at the academy. My jewellery is going to be showcased in the foyer.'

'Cool.' He nodded. 'That'll be great.'

Sophy's bubble of excitement popped. 'I just have to finish enough to mount a decent display.'

He looked at the table. 'This is where you work?'

'Sometimes I use the dining table, but it's easier in here.' Less mess for Rosanna.

His brows flickered, but then he looked at her. She knew

the subject had gone from his mind and something else was in its place. It was obvious—his body gave him away.

Lorenzo hadn't snuck out of a girl's room in years. Usually he could manage breakfast. He'd mastered the art of a sweet departure—a kiss, a smile, some lush words. But final. Always final.

But he didn't want to touch Sophy again. If he did, he knew he wouldn't be able to stop. And he refused to mess with her any more—although the reality was, she'd messed with *him*. He'd known it would be wild, but he hadn't thought he'd be filled with such awe. Be so moved by her. In truth, she scared him. How she made him feel scared him. She was so soft, so abandoned, so delicious.

She made him want more.

He carefully eased from her bed. She was lying in a sweet curve, her blonde curls spilling over the pillow. He resisted the urge to kiss her goodbye. He was hard again anyway. He didn't need to make it worse.

It was more nerve-racking then when he'd been trying to sneak out of the school dormitory with Alex crashing round behind him. It was all right for Alex—if he'd been caught it would have been a figurative rap on the knuckles. For Lorenzo it would have meant expulsion. He was always on that last chance. But then, as now, he made it.

He stood on the footpath outside her house and stretched, feeling the adrenalin surge through his muscles as he thought of their night together. He watched the dark sky start to lighten. Oh, yeah, as fantastic as it had been, he shouldn't have done it. Never, ever should have done it. And he sure as hell wasn't doing it again.

CHAPTER SIX

SOPHY opened her eyes when she heard the front door shut. She lay still a few moments longer just in case. Lorenzo had wanted to escape, she hadn't wanted to stop him. She figured he didn't want the awkward morning after either.

Had he even left a note? She rolled over, closing her mind to the slight tenderness of her body. No note—not on the pillow anyway. She lay on her back and looked up at the ceiling. Waited until she was sure he'd have driven away, then got up and walked into the lounge. The food was still on the table—all untouched. The only thing they'd eaten last night was each other. He'd had to come back out to the lounge at one point in the wee small hours to find the last couple of condoms that were hiding on the floor. And she was no girl scout—she *hadn't* been prepared for him. And she certainly wasn't prepared for this now. No regrets, but a nasty case of uncertainty.

She scraped the food into the bin, looked about as she worked. But there was no note anywhere else either.

And she had to face him at work in four hours' time.

She didn't bother going back to bed to try to get any more sleep. Instead she found her favourite navy trouser suit and made sure the shirt to wear beneath was pressed. She refused to let him ruffle her—not any more. But her heart thudded.

So they'd had their one night. And while she felt as if she'd died and gone to heaven, he obviously hadn't. He couldn't wait to get away—and hadn't wanted to deal with her. Okay, she'd get over that.

She really wished Rosanna were home. It wasn't her advice on how to get it that Sophy had needed. It was her advice on how to achieve a painless aftermath now. How did Rosanna keep on such good terms with all her old flames? And, even more importantly, how did she keep them all burning for her? Sophy shook her head—no, she didn't have either the secret or the skill for that.

Well, at the very least she'd try to borrow some Rosanna cool. She handled the boys with charm and smiles, right? Just made it easy for everyone. She winced. Sophy had made it easy for him all right. But he'd wanted her too, hadn't he? It hadn't been totally one-sided. She'd felt him shaking when he'd moved in her, she'd heard him growl with pleasure.

The balm from that reflection didn't last anywhere near long enough.

He just liked sex. It was obvious. It wasn't her he'd wanted, just the physical pleasure that she'd offered on a plate. What had she been thinking?

Okay, so the regrets were coming now—and the hurt that he hadn't felt anything special when she so totally had.

He wasn't in when she got there. Kat the receptionist said he'd be out most of the morning. Sophy was sure it was on purpose.

Fine.

She sat at the desk and did what she was famed for—getting on with the job. Organising everything. Victoria phoned, asking her to pick up some supplies from the deli for the dinner at their parents' place, and she had some meals to drop to Cara's house too—could Sophy do it?

Of course she could.

And in the end her nervous energy was wasted—he didn't show up at all. Sophy decided to leave early too. She'd cleared the backlog—there was no reason for her to be working full time hours any more. She'd stick with what she was good at. She did the errands for Victoria, then went to her parents' place for the catch-up. While there she did more, making herself feel useful—wanted by someone for something.

When she got to work the next day he was out again. Sophy bristled inside—really, wasn't he taking it a bit far? What was he afraid of? That she'd throw herself at him—*again*?

She winced. She *had* thrown herself at him. Not making that mistake again. Not ever. Hours later she hung up from her millionth call and looked up at a small sound.

He stood in the doorway, his face half in shadow. 'Everything okay?'

'Yes.' Sophy smiled. 'Of course.' She looked at the piles of paper in front of her. 'It's been a busy morning but I think I've got just about everything sorted now. Including all the details for the fundraising gig at the bar tomorrow night.'

'Great.' He hesitated.

She waited.

But he said nothing. So it was true that men never did want to talk about it. Well, she didn't want to either. What was the point? It was done. It was finished. She wasn't going to go all cold and wounded on him. But not flirty and desperate either. She'd aim for friendly professional. She flashed him a smile—just the right touch of warmth but not overly so. 'I'm off in a minute. I'll drop to part-time hours as we discussed now the backlog is cleared.'

He annoyed her completely by walking further into her office instead of hoofing off to his own as she'd hoped. She looked out of the window so she didn't have to look at him.

'The vandals have been back.' She'd noticed it this morning. The graffiti was huge—stunning, if Sophy dared offer her opinion, which she didn't because now he had that really brooding look on his face. 'You didn't hear them?' It had to have been more than one kid to spray a piece that big in a short time.

'I'm a deep sleeper,' he said dryly.

She shifted a letter unnecessarily. That was dangerous territory. 'What a pain for you to have to paint over it again.'

He shrugged. 'I'll leave it for a bit.'

'Fair enough.' She was quite pleased. She liked the colours, the whole fence looked on fire with the crimson reds and burnt gold coils.

She logged off the computer, gathered a couple of items to put back in the cabinet. It only took a moment. Then she reached for her favourite shiny handbag. Definitely time to make her exit.

Lorenzo leaned against the window frame and watched. Wow, she really was efficient, wasn't she? Had filed him away as if he were one of those pieces of paper. Checked him off her list and moved on. Forgotten about him.

And he shouldn't give a damn.

And he didn't—it was just his cock making things complicated. Leaping to attention when he merely walked the corridor—before he'd even seen her, let alone caught her fresh scent on the gentle breeze. The desire gnawed at him—had ruined his sleep last night. He'd lain awake, the noise of the city at night loud in his ears. So often it had soothed him. He'd spent so many nights listening to the traffic, imagining he was in one of those cars and just driving, driving, driving away.

And the restlessness had driven him outside—to the cover of darkness where he could create. Despite it being his property, it still thrilled him—helped release the anger that had burned in him since he could remember. Making his mark—he was there and they couldn't get rid of him, no matter how much they wanted to.

Alex had had a bit of bitterness with the mess his parents had made. Lorenzo was filled with it.

He'd chuckled as he worked on the fence. What would the do-good miss say if she knew it was him? He'd spent hours on it—switched all the lights in the warehouse on to cast a glow out to the yard. But in the end it hadn't done its job. Nor had the five-mile run he'd taken after. He was still angry. He was still frustrated.

He still burned inside.

But he'd discovered something that offered the softest respite from the old torment.

Sophy.

Unfortunately she was also the cause of half his trouble. Somehow just being around her—and her perfect looks, her proper manner—brought those old feelings back.

'You are coming to the fundraiser tomorrow night, aren't you?' he struggled to ask casually.

'You really need me to?'

'Yes.' Hell, yes. 'It would be good to have you on hand to make sure the information side of things goes smoothly.' He totally made it up. There was no information side of things.

'Then I'll be there.' She paused by the door on her way

out, turned back to look at him, an irritatingly benign smile on her face. 'I assume it's all right to bring a date?'

Every muscle locked onto red alert. A date? He had to force his jaw apart to answer. 'Of course.'

Rosanna flew back late Saturday afternoon. Sophy gave her an hour to relax in the bath then asked her as she lay on the sofa flicking through a magazine. 'You have to come out with me tonight.'

'And you're so desperate for my presence because?'

'I need your support.'

Rosanna tossed the magazine to the floor. 'What's happened?'

'Nothing. But I don't feel like walking into a crowded bar all by myself.'

'What bar?'

'Wildfire. Only opened this week. There's a fundraiser tonight for the Whistle Fund there. I have to go. But I don't want to go alone.'

'How is our favourite shark?'

Sophy shrugged. 'I hardly see him. He's very busy. He's the money behind this bar.'

'I'll text the boys. Spread the word. It should be fun. And it's for a good cause.' Rosanna leapt up into action. 'Well, we'd better find ourselves something suitable to wear, then, huh?'

Sophy grinned. Yeah, there was no holding Rosanna back from a party—or an excuse to get dressed to the nines. But two hours later she stared at her reflection in horror. 'I'm not wearing this.'

'Why not? You look hot.'

She looked like a wannabe catwoman, in Rosanna's favourite black—skin-tight satin pants and a sleek, sheer top. It smacked of trying too hard, too out of character—as if she were going out of her way to draw his attention. Which she wasn't. Not again. 'It's more you than me.'

'Keep the trousers, change the top.' Rosanna was working on her eyes.

Okay, that she could handle. Sophy went back to her own wardrobe and found one of her pretty silk tops—that flowed, less in your face figure-hugging. She picked up one of her necklaces.

Rosanna appeared in her doorway. 'Can I borrow one?'

'Absolutely.'

The bar was already packed when they got there. There was no formal aspect to the fundraiser. It was just that the charity was getting a percentage of the ticket sales—so, really, she didn't think she had to be there. But she couldn't not.

Yeah, the place was an instant success. Lorenzo had the Midas touch, didn't he? Knew the investments to pick, always had his finger on the new big thing.

Sophy let Rosanna lead the way to the bar, she had a way about her that parted crowds. They ordered—classic cocktails—and waited for them to be mixed. Rosanna flipped so her back was against the bar and surveyed the room. 'Looks good.'

Sophy nodded, trying not to look anywhere. She didn't want to see him. Didn't want to have to admit she had no date.

'Oh, my.' Rosanna sighed, fanning herself.

'What?'

'I just saw Lorenzo.'

'Oh.'

Rosanna spun back and leaned into Sophy. 'I just saw the way he was looking at you.'

'Oh?' Sophy's skin felt as if it were about to blister.

'Kitten you are going to be gobbled. One bite.' Rosanna laughed. 'Lucky kitty.'

'The jet lag is getting to you,' Sophy muttered, lifting the glass to her lips.

'Going to introduce me to your date, Sophy?'

She gulped, the liquid burning. Oh, there he was. Right behind her. She turned. In the crush of bodies at the bar he was too close.

'Of course.' She summoned some social skills. 'This is my very special friend Rosanna. Rosanna, this is Lorenzo.'

'Pleasure.' Lorenzo was purring like the cat who'd not just got the cream, but the bird too. 'Vance wanted to meet you too. He's my co-owner and manager of the bar.'

Lorenzo moved slightly closer to Sophy so the man behind him could be seen. Sophy felt Rosanna stiffen.

'Hi, Vance.' Sophy smiled, breaking the short silence.

But the newcomer wasn't looking at her. He was star-ing—hard—at Rosanna. And she was positively glaring back. They were squaring off like ancient enemies.

'Aren't you too old to still be dressing like a skateboard punk?' Rosanna was all snark.

'Aren't you too old to still have an eating disorder?' Vance answered ten degrees too coolly.

Sophy's jaw hit the floor. Rosanna was sleek, utterly sleek and stylish. But she wasn't sick. At least, Sophy didn't *think* so. And this guy so wasn't her type—she liked them with as much style as her own. Sophisticated style, not street wear. Although Vance had his strengths, to be sure.

'Do you two know each other already?' Sophy asked,

despite the obviousness of the answer. It wasn't normal to be trading insults so soon in an acquaintance.

Rosanna didn't even glance at her. 'We met a few years ago.'

'Come and dance, Sophy.' Lorenzo grabbed her hand in a death grip, took the glass from her other and ditched it on the bar, marching her away despite her protests.

'Hey, I'd hardly had any of that.'

'I'll get you another later.'

She pulled to slow him, twisted back to catch another glimpse of Rosanna. 'Do you think they're okay? They look like they might kill each other.'

'I think they'll be okay. She's all grown-up.'

Sophy really wasn't so sure. She tugged her arm again. 'She's not as tough as she makes out.'

Lorenzo laughed, the glint in his eyes too dangerous for comfort. 'She'll be fine. Forget about it.'

Well, she wasn't going to do that. 'She's my friend.'

'Just give them five minutes.' He looked at her, the darkness in him piercing now. 'Or is it that you don't want to dance with me?'

She went cool, despite the thudding in her heart. 'I like dancing.'

'Right.'

The music was loud—if they were to hear each other they'd have to lean close. Sophy opted for silence. But he was too close anyway, moving closer. And she couldn't cope with the way his big body moved—with surprising grace—or the way he absorbed the beat so naturally.

She felt increasingly stilted, her pulse skipping—too fast for the rhythm of the music. She couldn't relax—tried not to look at him at all. Until he grasped her by the upper arms and pulled her to him.

She gasped as their bodies collided.

'You're mad with me for leaving like that,' he roughly muttered in her ear.

'No, I'm not.' She shook head and glared at him. 'It was good you did, actually.'

'Oh?' His eyes glittered in the lights. It looked as if his temper was off the leash now.

'Saved us from any awkwardness,' she snapped.

'And you're not awkward now?'

'No.' She tossed her head, refusing to admit she was basically dying of discomfort. 'But my shoes are killing me so I've had enough dancing, thanks. You don't need me for anything tonight anyway, right? For the Whistle, I mean.'

'No.' His reply was frigid. Hard eyes raked her. 'Not at all.' He pushed her away and stalked through the crowd.

Sophy felt her own anger grow. What did he want—for her to fall at his feet again? To act the desperate female?

Never.

She pushed her way back to the bar where Rosanna was standing alone—a fresh cocktail in hand. She handed it out and Sophy gladly took a deep sip and handed it back.

'Why don't you just do him and be done with it?' Rosanna asked as if it were the most logical thing in the world. 'Honestly, the tension between you two is electric.'

Sophy didn't inform her that she already had done him. And that instead of making the tension go away it had only made it worse. Much, *much* worse.

'I should have known you'd have it in you. You never give yourself enough credit, as a result no one else does,' Rosanna commented. 'Our mistake.'

Have what in her? The ability to attract a shark like Lorenzo? Big deal. Rosanna had been right first time round—she couldn't handle him. 'What's with you and the

Vance guy?' Sophy asked, wanting to think about something else. 'I mean, that was rude, even for you.'

Rosanna shrugged. 'Unfinished business, you know?'

Um, well, yes. Sophy knew Rosanna was angry, but she had her own frustrations too—and she needed space to deal with them. 'I've had enough. I'm going home. You coming?'

Rosanna had the huntress look in her eye. 'No. I'm finishing the business. Tonight.'

'Are you sure?' Sophy didn't think it was such a good idea. Rosanna rarely allowed her emotions to bubble close to the surface and right now they were clearly on show.

'Deadly.'

Sophy hesitated, wondered if she should stay—convince her friend to let it go. But she felt the presence at her back—the surge in awareness. She turned. Lorenzo—standing a millimetre away but looking totally remote. And she just knew he'd been listening in.

'Stuck for a ride?' he asked bluntly.

'I can get a cab.'

'No need. I'll run you home.'

'You're not staying?'

'Obviously not.'

She hesitated. It would be churlish to refuse. And she was handling this like a sophisticate, wasn't she? 'That would be great. Thanks.'

They walked from the bar. Not awkward at all? Ha.

'It's a real success,' she said for the sake of saying something.

'Yeah. Vance had the vision. It was a good one.'

But it was Lorenzo who had backed him on it. Kat had told her some of the background—turned out Lorenzo was the only one who would back Vance, when the banks wouldn't.

'I wonder how Rosanna knows him.'

'You'll have to ask her.'

Quite the clam, wasn't he? She gave up on the small talk and simply watched him drive. The powerful machine purred under his hands, responding to his slightest touch. Just as she had. She started to sweat again, clenched her muscles to stop the softening. She still wanted him, *badly*. But she wasn't going to make the mistake of asking him again—she didn't want to hear him say no. He pulled over outside Rosanna's villa. She undid her belt and had her door open in a split second. The sooner she got away from him, the more likely she was to escape with the little dignity she had left. But her deeply ingrained politeness made her bend and glance back into the car—right at him. 'Thanks for the ride.'

'My pleasure.' His hard gaze bored into her.

Utterly still, she took in the intensity in his face. Why so angry? Burning with confusion, with embarrassment as she suddenly thought of an alternative to the 'ride' they were talking about, she slammed the door.

Lorenzo swore. Forced himself to wait until she was inside the door of her home and then put his foot to the floor. What the hell was he doing hovering around her? She was determined not to be bothered, that their night truly was all over. She couldn't have made that clearer. And wasn't that what he wanted?

No. He'd wanted her to admit she was feeling as out of sorts as he was—as unfulfilled, as hungry.

He gripped the wheel tighter and knew he'd better head back to the warehouse pronto before he did something stupid. He could feel it surging within him, the energy seeking to burst out of his skin. He hadn't felt it this bad in a long time—the anger and the desire to destroy. The darkness deep within him was awake. Maybe it was a result of the illness last week. His control had been weakened. But it was the thought of Sophy that threatened it the most.

He'd just stay up all night. He'd get it back under control.

CHAPTER SEVEN

ROSANNA didn't return that night but sent a safe-status text in the morning. Sophy grumped her way through breakfast, telling herself she desperately needed to Get Over Lorenzo.

She stayed at home all Sunday but went to work her usual ten minutes early on Monday. Tried to keep her pulse at a vaguely normal rate as she climbed the stairs up to her little domain. Not awkward. Not awkward at all.

She heard the voices as she neared the top. Stopped on the threshold of her office door. The girl was very pretty. Already seated in *Sophy's* chair. Kat, the receptionist, was showing her the damn computer system already.

'Hello.' Sophy smiled, ultra bright and polite. She was not going to get evil over this.

'Hi, Sophy.' Kat looked up and beamed. 'This is Jemma, who's here to help you out.'

Oh, right. Help her out. Like she needed helping out? Like she needed a pretty, petite thing to do the work for her? Oh, please. After she'd just spent the last week giving the place a complete overhaul? She didn't need help *now*. No, it was more like now the hard stuff was done she wasn't needed any more.

Now he'd slept with her he didn't want her around at all.

It wouldn't be awkward at all then, would it?

The jealousy kicked in, the resentment swirling around, the energy building in her until she had enough fuel inside to launch a rocket to the moon.

'Are you okay showing her some stuff for a while longer, Kat?' she barely managed to ask nicely.

Kat nodded.

'Great.' Yes, she wasn't needed at all. She gripped her bag all the more tightly. 'I've just got to see Lorenzo.'

Kat nodded. 'He's about. I saw him earlier.'

Oh, good. Sophy briskly walked the few metres along the corridor to his office—it was empty. She checked the other office—the other staff were back now, having done their bit for Vance. But Lorenzo wasn't in with them either. She walked faster—she refused to let him avoid this one.

She went downstairs but he wasn't out in the yard. She went into one of the darkened rooms where they stored the cases of wine—all on pallets ready to be shipped. He was bending down by one, checking the dispatch label by the looks of things. He straightened when he saw her. Watched as she walked towards him, the heels of her shoes rapidly clicking on the concrete floor.

'You've got a temp in,' she said briskly.

'Yeah.'

Even though she knew already, she had to take a second to absorb the hit from the casual dismissal in his tone.

'I thought you were all about keeping Cara happy and not getting some clueless temp in?' Sophy cringed even as she bitched at him; she was quite sure Jemma wasn't clueless, but it had been his point originally. 'Do you have any idea how hard I've worked here? I've fixed the whole mess.'

'I know you have. A five-year-old could work the filing system you've put in place. It's perfect for a temp now.'

She reeled. Was that supposed to be a compliment? To make her feel okay about it? 'You mean it's the perfect time to get rid of me.'

He walked towards her. 'What are you so mad about? I thought there were other things you wanted to be doing anyway?'

That wasn't the point. The point was his shabby treatment of her. 'You just don't want me to be here any more? You're embarrassed. You're the one who's feeling awkward.'

'That's not why I got a temp in.'

'Yeah, right. Can't handle it, can you? Anything remotely personal going on in your precious little domain.'

'What happened with us is not why she's here.'

'That's rubbish, Lorenzo. At least be honest and admit it. You want me gone.'

He swore right back at her—only worse. 'Quite the opposite. Come with me.'

Given he now had hold of her wrist in a clench that threatened to break the smallest bones in there, she didn't have much choice.

'Lorenzo!'

He didn't listen. Didn't stop. Stormed out of the store room and up the stairs, past the offices until he got to the empty room at the back.

He let her go and she was still moving so fast from being dragged along with him she half ran into the middle of the room. He strode back to the door and slammed it shut, whirled to face her, his arms flung out. 'This is why.'

She stared around the big empty room. There was a large table in the middle, a few chairs around it. 'I don't follow.'

Clearly fuming, he enlightened her. 'You can set up in here. Work the rest of the day, half the night if you need to. To get your jewellery done for the show. This can be your workroom.'

She stared at him. 'You're kidding.'

'No.' He walked further into the room, turned his back to her so she couldn't read his expression. 'I'm vaguely useful. If you need to use power tools or something, I can help.'

'You mean you can plug them in?'

He grunted then—almost a laugh. 'Yeah.' He faced her, his hands on his hips, still looking like a warrior about to launch an offensive any minute. 'I just thought you could work here in the afternoons. You'd be around if the temp needed help but you'd have the time to work on your own stuff. You can stay later. You don't have to pack it up at the end of the day, just spread out and get it done.'

Calm descended over her, her earlier anger soothed by a new suspicion. 'Why didn't you tell me?'

He looked even grumpier. 'It was supposed to be a surprise.'

She blinked. Well, it had been a surprise. But he'd meant it as a *nice* surprise. 'Why did you want to surprise me?'

He looked away. 'I don't know.'

Yes, he did. She waited.

'You've done a lot for the fund,' he muttered. 'I thought it was a way of saying thanks.'

And that was all it was? She didn't think so. She walked right into his personal space, her heart hurtling inside but trying to keep her efficient cool look on the outside.

He stiffened but didn't move away.

'Did you want to do something nice for me, Lorenzo?'

He looked to the side but still didn't step back.

She smiled and took another pace closer. And closer still.

His hands were suddenly on her arms. 'What are you doing?'

'I thought I'd say thank you,' she breathed oh-so-innocently.

His gaze dropped to her lips. His fingers tightened that extra notch but the rest of him stayed rigid.

Bingo.

The guy still wanted.

Well, the guy would get.

But not yet.

She reached up on tiptoe, brushed her lips ever so gently against his jaw—that inch too close to his lips to be purely platonic as he had once done to her. She stayed there a second longer, whispered in a way she'd only ever fantasised about, 'Thank you, Lorenzo.'

She tried to move back but his hands were keeping her there now. 'Sophy.'

Part warning, part what? Sophy couldn't decide. But the whisper seemed to have gone down quite well.

He sighed—part groan—and his fingers softened, smoothing over her skin. 'You smell good.'

'Do I?'

He nodded. 'I smell you everywhere.'

'Cheap shampoo. Everyone uses it.'

'No,' he half laughed. 'It's you. Only you. And you don't use cheap shampoo.'

Oh, that was nice. She let her weight rest against him a little more.

'If we do this again, and I mean *if*, then no one knows,' he said firmly.

'What, it's our "little secret"?' She pulled back to look at him. She wouldn't have thought he'd be one to care.

'I'm not having gossip on site. No one is to know.'

'So we remain professional through the day and meet up for rabid sex at night? Is that it?'

His whole body tensed.

She stepped closer, her confidence blossoming despite his obviously conflicted feelings. At least it meant he had feelings. 'Let's get one other thing straight, Lorenzo. If we do this again, and I mean *if*, then it's for more than one night.'

He swallowed.

'We're not done until it's finished,' she told him quietly. She was not having another couple of days like this. She'd work him right out of her system. She'd had a taste of danger and she wanted to take it all until there was no danger left.

'But it will finish.'

'Sure.' She nodded. It was serious physical chemistry, that was all. She'd get her stuff done for the exhibition and be able to walk away. A week or so would be enough to neutralise it. 'Deal?'

He nodded. 'Come upstairs with me now.' His hands were seeking already, sliding beneath the hem of her clothing, hunting for bare skin.

'I thought you didn't want to have sex here?' What about gossip onsite? Hell if any of them came looking for either of them now they'd be in trouble.

'I've changed my mind.'

As his hot gaze drank her in she could read his thoughts and she struggled to stay calm.

She put her palm on his flushed cheek. 'What about Kat? And Jemma and the others?'

He closed his eyes. 'Sophy.' He sounded so tormented.

She reached up. 'I want you.' She kissed him. His arms tightened and he didn't let her free of the kiss. But his tension eased, his hands stroking with care now. So that had been what he needed. How surprising—so the neediness wasn't all her? She could feel his heart pounding against her. Maybe they could go upstairs—sneak up there now just quickly.

Her phone rang. And rang and rang.

Sophy broke the kiss. 'I have to get that,' she muttered.

He looked at her, bitterness flashing on his face. 'Of course you do.'

She scrabbled in her bag to find the phone at the bottom, smoothed her hair behind her ears, quickly inhaled to cover her breathlessness and put a smile on her face so her greeting would sound friendly. 'Sophy speaking.'

He watched her, his face as readable as a stone. She flashed a wider smile at him.

'Hi, Ted, what's up?' She swung away as she listened. 'And you need me to pick it up? Sure. No problem. Give me the address.' She dug back into the bag for a pen—no point asking her brother to text the details; he would say he didn't have the time. Sophy repeated the address back to him, glanced up in time to see Lorenzo walking out of the room. Two minutes later the call was dealt with. Sophy stared at the door, wondering why he'd gone.

She went back into her office—found Kat had left Jemma figuring out stuff on her own.

'It's great you're here.' Sophy smiled, meaning it this time.

But Jemma's attention wasn't on her. She was looking out of the window.

Thud, thud, thud.

Sophy didn't need to look to know what it was but she did anyway. He was back out there already bouncing his damn ball. Well, she wasn't going to go running after him, not this time. She looked across and frowned at the fence. It was covered in even more graffiti now.

She didn't see him the rest of the day, didn't expect to

see him until the next. But when her doorbell rang she wasn't surprised.

'Have you eaten?' she asked as she opened it to let him in.

He was leaning against the door jamb. Dressed entirely in dark clothes—black trousers, a charcoal V-neck tee. 'That's not why I'm here.'

She deliberately leaned against the opposite side of the door frame. 'No? Then why are you here?'

'Don't play games.' His glare blistered. So he was still brooding.

'You'd better come in.'

He crossed the threshold into the hall, stopped as he saw the black-clad sylph standing at the other end of the hall.

'Lorenzo, you met Rosanna the other night. Rosanna, this is Lorenzo, my boss.'

His frown super-sized up.

Rosanna moved swiftly down the hall, her case rolling behind her. 'I'm off, darling. Back in a few days. Be good.' She grinned wickedly.

'You too,' Sophy tried to coo, but it was a squeak.

She heard Rosanna's chuckle.

Lorenzo was still frowning long after the door had closed behind Rosanna.

'She's very discreet,' Sophy said to reassure him. 'She won't say anything.'

He jerked his head to the side. 'I'm not your boss.'

Oh, was that the problem? She smiled. 'Yes you are.'

'Not really.'

She knew what he meant and this was different from the usual office affair. In truth she was doing him a favour working for Whistle. The balance of power wasn't so weighted towards him—at least not in respect of that. Sophy wanted to smooth it even more. 'Tell you what, why don't you let me be the boss in the bedroom—that'll even us out.'

'Never.' The fire in his eyes burned from ice-cold to hot.

'But it's my bedroom.'

He shook his head, chasing off the last of the threatening storm clouds.

'You just see if you can stay in charge, then. *Boss.*' She threw down the challenge. Knew she didn't have a hope in winning at all—but shrieked with laughter as she turned and ran as fast as she could to her room.

He caught her before she got there and went completely caveman. And she was quite happy to be his woman of the moment.

The days couldn't pass fast enough. He was on her doorstep before she even got home some nights. But he didn't suggest she ride home with him and nor did she offer to take him. The boundaries might be invisible but they were there.

But as the evenings lengthened and their physical need was temporarily tamed she turned and talked to him. About nothing. About everything. But never about anything personal. She didn't want to talk about her family, sensed he never would talk about his. But one night she got some courage and steered the conversation slightly towards him. 'Why the Whistle Fund?'

He lifted his head off the pillow. 'Why at all?'

'No, why the name?'

'Because that's what you do when you need help. You whistle.' He pursed his lips and gave a short whistle.

'And you whistle so you're not afraid—there's a song about that.'

'Yeah, and when you're doing something you shouldn't,

you have a mate keeping lookout—who'll whistle if you need to make a run for it.'

She laughed at that. 'Did you need to make a run for it often?'

'All the time.' He grinned.

She laughed with him but wasn't at all sure how much he meant it as a joke. 'And you whistle at pretty women, right?'

'Oh, no,' he said mock soberly. 'That's not pc.'

'You're not pc.' She rolled onto her tummy. 'Have there been many women Lorenzo?'

'Are you sure this is a conversation you want to have?'

The coolness was almost visible. Damn it, why shouldn't they talk about their pasts? Couldn't they have a laugh about the mistakes they'd made before? Why was he blocking her from getting to know anything more about him? She'd heard the little there was to hear. So his childhood hadn't been a picnic, okay, she'd gathered that. But he'd gone to that great school hadn't he? Someone had cared enough to pay for that. And he'd become amazingly successful.

'Why not? Tell me about your first and worst, I'll tell you about mine.'

'Look, we're meeting up for the *occasional* screw. That doesn't mean we're going to swap life secrets or play twenty questions.'

Sophy flinched. Every night wasn't exactly occasional. Jerk. Her temper flared. 'Touchy, aren't you? What happened? Did you fall in love once? Did she reject you—did she say you weren't good enough for her? The poor boy from the wrong side of the tracks?' Sarcasm flavoured every mean little word.

He sat up and pushed the sheet from him. 'Actually I rejected her.'

'Oh,' Sophy said. 'Of course. Silly me. You like to do that, don't you? And why did you? Did she want too much from you?'

He swung his legs off the bed, turned his back to her. This time she had it right. The anger rippled through his muscles.

'Poor Lorenzo, someone actually wanting emotional commitment? Support, honesty, love?'

'Nothing so devastating,' he denied. 'She no longer turned me on.'

Sophy blinked. Ouch. There was a warning. She got out of bed too, pulled a shirt over her cold arms. She didn't want him to be with her all night now. Not tonight.

'You know, I have lots of work to do.' She let her gaze slide over her desk—it was covered with designs and half-finished pieces that she'd decided weren't going to go in the show. But he didn't know that.

He looked at the table, then at her. 'You want me to leave?'

Sophy forced a shrug. 'Rosanna's back in town, she'll probably be home soon.'

'And you don't want her to know how loud I can make you come.'

She coloured. She supposed she deserved it. She was being rude chucking him out. 'I wouldn't be able to come with anyone right next door.'

'Really.' His sarcasm practically splashed on the floor. He pulled on his tee shirt and jeans.

He was angry—the way he moved totally gave it away. Well, so was she.

He didn't kiss her goodbye. Just strode out. She didn't speak—just slipped into the lounge and watched from the window as he jogged down to his car. But to her surprise he didn't get into it and drive off. Instead he kept on jogging, his pace picking up to a hard-out run. In the darkened room she kept an eye on the street. It was a good forty minutes later before he returned. His tee shirt sweat darkened in patches. He didn't look at the house, stayed too focused on his car for it to be natural as he unlocked and slid into it. The engine roared. He was at the speed limit in a second.

Sophy usually spent an hour each morning working with Jemma making sure the girl had a good grasp of the processes. She did—she certainly wasn't clueless. Then Sophy left and went into her mini workshop. Her heart sank as she saw the volume of work she still had to do. Her confidence had dipped—none of it was good enough to go on display. She was totally fooling herself. She was going to embarrass herself completely. Her mobile went and she answered right away—glad of the excuse to turn her back on the mess. She listened. 'Sure, I'll come right away.'

She met him on the stairs on the way out.

'Where are you going?' His super-size frown was back.

'I've promised my mother I'd meet her to help with something at lunch.'

'But you're supposed to be making your jewellery. You've still got several pieces unfinished.' He climbed to the stair just below hers.

'I know,' she said, pausing for a second to wonder how *he* knew—had he been poking around in her room up there? 'But I promised.'

He looked angrier than he had when he'd left last night. He stretched his hands out to the rails either side of the stairs so he made a wall she somehow had to get past. 'But you've only got a week 'til the show.'

She knew that too. 'I'll work on them later.'

His eyes narrowed. 'You don't want to do it, do you? The exhibition.'

'What? Of course I do.'

'If you did you'd be prioritising it.'

She stiffened at the implied criticism. 'Things other than work have priority in my life, Lorenzo. *People* have priority.' Which was more than could be said for him. As far as she could tell he lived for work and work alone. People—*relationships*—didn't feature in the equation at all. 'My mother has asked for help. I'm pleased to be able to.'

'No, she could get someone else. It's just that you can't say no when someone asks you. It wouldn't matter if it was her or anyone.'

'And that's a bad thing?' She glared at him.

'It is when it stops you from achieving your own dreams.'

'Like I said, people come first for me, Lorenzo. Always.'

'Aren't you a person? Isn't what you want just as valid as what others want? Surely if you explained how busy you were, she'd find someone else to do whatever it is. A paid assistant, perhaps?'

She stiffened—but not because of the little jibe.

His eyes narrowed. 'She doesn't know, does she?' With scary precision he zoomed in on the problem.

No, and Sophy didn't want her to—didn't want any of them to. 'The sooner I go and do this, the sooner I can get back upstairs.'

'But you were out yesterday afternoon too. For three hours.'

What was he, her timesheet? She wasn't accountable to him. Not on this.

'You can't let this opportunity go, Sophy. Your work is too good.'

That made her even more tense—she felt pressure enough without him making sweet comments like that. 'I really have to go, Lorenzo.' She looked past him down the stairs. 'And it really isn't any of your business.' He wouldn't open up to her at all, so why should he have the right to comment on her life?

'Sophy,' he said quietly, leaning forward and branding her lips with the heat of his. 'At least be quick.'

CHAPTER EIGHT

'SOPHY, can you come with me, please?' Lorenzo met her as she walked into the building.

She glanced at Kat behind the reception desk, hoping the girl hadn't picked up on the chill in his words. 'Of course.'

Was he mad with her? She hadn't returned to the warehouse yesterday—had got held up completely until the early evening. Her sister had come round and it had turned into a whole family gathering. She'd made excuses and gone after a while—but she needn't have hurried. Lorenzo hadn't come round, had left no message on her phone. It was the first night they hadn't had sex all week. And stupidly she'd had less sleep than ever. So she really wasn't in the mood to have a hard time from him.

He led her out the back and gestured for her to get into his car.

'Where are we going?' She fixed her seat belt—he already had the engine running.

'You'll see.' He fiddled with the stereo and put the music up loud. What, he didn't want conversation?

'I had a nice night, thanks.' She chit chatted really loudly just to annoy him. He didn't want to talk personal? Tough. 'Big dinner with my parents and Victoria and Ted. It's my niece's birthday this weekend so we were celebrating early. Rosanna sent a text. She's in Sydney for a few days.'

He gave her a sideways look but said nothing.

Yeah, she loved having conversations by herself. So she gave up. They drove through half of Auckland and she relaxed into the comfortable seat. Suddenly she sat up. 'Lorenzo, this is the airport.'

'And we're right on time.'

On time for what? 'Where are we going?'

'Have you ever gotten on a plane and not known the destination?'

She shook her head.

'Now's your chance.'

'Lorenzo—'

'Have you ever taken a risk? Gone with an impulse?'

'Maybe,' she said cautiously. Like the time she'd come on to him with the basketball.

He parked the car, crossed his arms and called her on it. 'What are you going to do, Sophy? Play it safe or walk on the wild side? Come on an adventure.'

'How wild an adventure?'

'Totally legal.' He rolled his eyes. 'Honestly, don't make a big deal about it, you'll end up disappointed.'

She didn't think so. She didn't think she'd ever be disappointed when he was offering adventure.

He got out of the car. 'Are you coming or what?'

As if she could say no. He loaded a surprisingly heavy-looking suitcase onto a trolley and headed to the check-in. She wasn't worried. It wasn't as if they were going to go overseas—he didn't have her passport, this was the domestic terminal.

'We're flying back tonight, right?' She'd better check on that though.

'No.'

'Then when?'

'Sunday.'

Sunday? 'Lorenzo, I can't. I promised my brother I'd organise the cupcakes for my niece's party.'

'Were you going to bake them?'

'They're not that hard.' She nibbled her lower lip. 'Oh, I can't, Lorenzo. I can't let him down. I can't let her down.' But she was disappointed for herself more than anything.

'Do you have to be at the party?'

'No. It's for her little friends. I was just making the cakes. She likes the icing I do.'

'Someone else can do icing.'

Who? Baking wasn't something anyone else in her family did.

'Phone a bakery and get them to deliver,' Lorenzo said, as if he were instructing a small child. He was right, of course. It would be so easy.

'It's short notice.'

'Just offer to pay double and they'll do it.'

She laughed. 'Is that how you get what you want? Offer to pay?'

'No. That wouldn't work with you. I have to come up with other alternatives.' He grinned. 'Like abduction.'

She chomped on her lip some more. So tempted.

'Phone up and get it done.' He gave her a sideways look. 'What else did you have scheduled for the weekend?'

'A few things.' Sophy dug out her phone and her diary. 'What am I going to tell them?'

'The truth.'

'I don't want to.'

'You don't want to say you're running off for a dirty long weekend?'

Oh, she couldn't hesitate now. 'We're a secret, remember?'

She got on and made the calls. It took the whole twenty minutes they had left on the ground to rearrange everything she'd agreed to do in the weekend.

She put the phone away but her practical-oriented brain presented her with the next set of problems.

He lifted her face to his. 'What's wrong now?'

'I don't have any clothes with me.'

'You don't need any.'

'Oh, we're going to a naturist colony? Awesome.' She aimed for sarcastic but was burning inside with the naughty promise of his words. 'They don't mind furry teeth either?'

He laughed. 'There are shops where we're going. We can get you a toothbrush, okay?'

'Fabulous.'

The flight was only just over an hour. Christchurch. She knew the destination now, of course—the signs and the pilot's message had given that one away. She was fine with it. Christchurch was a nice city and she hadn't been there in ages.

But when they got into the rental car he headed straight onto the bypass and the motorway north.

'Where are we going?'

'I told you, you'll see.'

After forty minutes or so she thought she had it figured. The rows and rows of vines in the fields gave it away. Waipara—part of the wine region.

'We're staying on a vineyard?'

'No.' He kept driving.

It was another hour, passing alongside a river and the weird shaped cabbage trees that looked like something Dr Seuss would have drawn. A few sheep were scattered in the fields. And then they got there—to Hanmer Springs, an Alpine spa town in the heart of a geo-thermal area. He slowed down as they drove through the main street of the village.

'Look, swimsuit shop on the right,' he pointed out. 'Leopard print number in the window gets my vote.'

Oh, please.

'Superette on the left for toothpaste and other essentials.' He pointed with his hand. 'Bakery for the best pies in the country.'

She chuckled. 'Everything one could possibly need.'

'That's right. Now I'm going back to Waipara for some meetings.' Halfway up the hill he pulled up in front of a house. 'You're staying here.'

She got out of the car. He was leaving her? She walked up the path slowly, not caring enough to appreciate the pretty wooden chalet he'd just unlocked. When was she getting the 'dirt' in the weekend? Inside he'd opened the big suitcase. Carefully packed inside was all her gear—all her tools, all her unfinished work. She stared at it, then at him.

'I'm not letting you throw away this opportunity, Sophy,' he said softly, placing his hands on her shoulders. 'Not even for hot sex with me.'

'Lorenzo—'

'Give me your phone.' He held out his hand.

She pulled it from her purse and gave it to him.

He switched it off and put it in his pocket. 'You have no excuses now. You have to finish them.' His expression softened. 'I've booked you into the spa at four p.m. for a massage and whatever other treatments you feel like.'

'Really?' Her spirits lifted a fraction.

'Uh-huh.' His eyes twinkled. 'But you have to do nothing, and I mean nothing, but work until then—deal?'

'Okay.'

'And you'll have to walk down to the spa because I'm taking the car.'

'That's okay.' She nodded again. 'Thanks.'

But she was disappointed. She *ached* for him. And he'd played on that—used it to set her up. She'd cleared her weekend to be with him, but now she had nothing to do but finish her pieces for the show.

She supposed she'd thank him one day.

He kissed her, drew away way too soon. But at least he groaned as he did. He put his hands behind his back. 'Nothing but work. *Nothing.*'

She managed a laugh and watched him go. As he got to the car she couldn't stop herself calling after him through the open door. 'You'll be back later?'

'Count on it.'

She turned back inside and looked at her stuff. She had all afternoon. All day Saturday and Sunday too. With no phone, no outside contact—no one calling. Suddenly she felt it—liberation. And she did as he'd bid. It only took twenty minutes to set herself up and then she worked. In the silence, alone, she got into the zone. Her enthusiasm for it returned, as did her confidence. She studied her options, assessing the work she had completed and her pages of notes for other styles. She deliberated carefully before making a decision. She wanted her work to be thematically linked, but for each piece to stand uniquely, to showcase a broad range.

There was a harsh ringing. She literally jumped three feet in the air. Spun round, looking for the source of the noise. It was the landline of the holiday home. 'Hello?'

'You need to go now or you'll miss your appointment.'

'Oh.' She looked at her watch. 'Is it that time already?'

He chuckled. 'You've been hard at it, haven't you?'

She leaned against the bench and let the smile out. 'Yes. Thank you.' She meant it this time.

It was a ten minute walk down the hill to the thermal pool complex, but she jogged it in five—so she had time to pick up a swimsuit from the store first. She walked straight past the leopard print but stopped at the rack of crimson costumes. There was a two piece the exact shade of part of the graffiti piece on Lorenzo's fence. She grabbed the one in her size—hoped the cut would be okay. She paid and ran—not wanting to be late.

She went for the full facial, full massage option. An hour and a half of pure bliss. At the end she couldn't have peeled herself off the table if she'd tried. The beautician left her to relax. Her private room had its own small pool of thermally heated, mineral-laden, olive-green water for her to melt into at her leisure. When she regained some kind of muscle control, that was.

She was almost asleep, lying on her tummy, when she heard him.

'Are you ready for your massage, ma'am?'

She smiled. She recognised the thread in that voice. 'I've already had my massage, thanks.'

'This one is a little special.'

She felt his hands circling over her back.

'Crimson,' he muttered. 'Good choice.'

She didn't roll over—for one thing she couldn't, for another she didn't want him to see how slight the triangles covering her breasts were. Not yet anyway—she was still getting used to them herself.

But he couldn't have been that into the bikini because in less than a minute he was pushing the briefs down. He lifted her foot, then the other to get the garment off—and when he placed each foot back he spread them a little further apart. Slid his hands hard up her calves, up the backs of her thighs…

She bit her lip, anticipation flooding her. 'Lorenzo, there are people everywhere.'

'I locked the door.' His 'massage' took an incredibly intimate turn.

'They'll hear us,' she said breathlessly.

'No, they'll hear *you*.' He laughed and bent to nip her butt while his thumbs stroked into the space between. 'Of course,' he added thoughtfully, 'you don't *have* to come. Women don't have to orgasm every time, do they? You can still enjoy sex regardless, right? It won't bother me.'

'How magnanimous of you.' She clutched the towel beneath her and tilted up to give him better access. It was one hell of a massage.

He murmured, mouth moist on her skin as he manipulated her—faster, deeper. 'Think of it as a challenge. I dare you not to come.'

She rocked, pushing harder onto him, her voice leaping three octaves. 'I can't not!'

He whipped his hands away and flipped her over. He was already naked, and in a moment was above her. He held her face hard between his hands, kissing her savagely while he surged into her. Her scream came out in another way—her fingernails raking down his back. He arched harder, his thrusts even more powerful.

It made it even better.

'Does anyone know about the show?'

They were in the water, cheeks flushed from the heat, bodies floating.

'Only Rosanna,' Sophy answered lazily. 'She got me the chance. One of her flirts sponsors the film festival.'

'And no one else?'

'No.'

'Sophy.'

'What?' She gazed at him candidly. 'It's not like you're an open book, Lorenzo. You keep everything from everybody.'

He frowned. 'Only the bad stuff.'

What, his whole life was bad? She just didn't believe that.

'Why don't you want to tell your family?' he asked.

'I'm going to. But I want them to see the stuff first—so I can see what they really think. And not just be nice because they know it was made by me.'

'What they think matters that much to you?'

'Sure,' she said. 'They're my family.'

He went quiet.

'I want them to be proud of me.' She tried to explain.

'There's no way they're not proud of you already.'

She smiled. But he was wrong. She'd let them down. 'I'm not like them.' But she didn't explain it further. Rather she let her hands slide over him—her reward for a long day of hard work. 'You were wrong.'

'What about?'

'This just can't be legal.'

He laughed.

'I'm serious. It feels too good.'

'I've got a secret for you, honey,' he whispered into her mouth. 'Only the things that are right feel this good.'

And that was the moment her heart liquefied. She tipped her head back to look up at him—a long, searching look. But his gaze slid from her and then the rest of him did.

He splashed up the steps out of the pool. 'We need to get moving.'

'You've got to be kidding.'

'A couple of my growers are coming in to Hanmer and we're going out to dinner.'

'What, like at a restaurant?'

'Yeah.' He turned on the shower.

'And it's okay for me to turn up in my bikini?'

He laughed under the stream of water. 'Absolutely.'

'Well, what else am I going to wear? My crushed suit from today?'

She was *naked*.

He left the shower running for her and wrapped a towel round his hips. While under the hot jet she watched him open his backpack. He pulled out another pair of jeans and tossed them on the massage table for her.

She switched off the water. 'I'm not going to meet people wearing your clothes.'

'Sophy—' he sent her a look '—relax. It's not a fancy restaurant. Just nice people, nice food.'

It *was* a fancy restaurant and wearing nothing but a pair of men's jeans that hung on her and a tourist tee shirt from the spa shop wasn't her idea of fancy restaurant attire. And, worse, wearing his jeans turned her on.

'Hi, Lorenzo. You must be Sophy.' So he'd mentioned her to them? She felt an absurdly warm glow about that.

To her relief the older couple were in jeans too and were full of welcoming smiles. Lorenzo explained that Charlotte and Rob Wilson had one of the largest holdings that supplied grapes to one of his labels. They were led to a table, talk turned to food and wine and business.

'Have you known Lorenzo long?' Sophy just had to do some digging while Lorenzo and Rob talked about the bar.

'Fifteen years,' Charlotte replied.

Sophy nearly spilt her wine. Wow—if there was someone who knew him it was this woman.

Charlotte was smiling at her as if she'd just read her mind. 'He used to work as a hand in the picking season. Right from when he was a teen and had nowhere to go in the holidays.' She looked at Sophy. 'I tried to spoil him but he wouldn't have it. I'd leave baking in his cabin and hope he got it. The tin was always empty when he left so I figured he did. Later on Alex used to come and work too. It was more fun for him then, I think.'

Sophy swallowed. 'He was lucky he worked with you.'

'He worked on another vineyard when he was still at school too. The McIntosh property.' Charlotte shook her head. 'I've never known someone to be so driven to succeed. And he has.'

Yeah, but was he happy with it? Sophy was increasingly worried there was a huge depth of unhappiness in him.

'Now he's invested in this bar. Who knows what he'll turn to next? He's a natural entrepreneur. He's a genius.'

Okay, so Charlotte was his number one fan.

'What are you talking about?' Lorenzo turned to them.

'You.' Charlotte smiled at him. 'When are you going to be satisfied, Lorenzo?'

'I don't want to get bored.'

Sophy smiled as the woman laughed. But her nerves stretched. Bored—as he had been with the woman who'd no longer turned him on? He was busy—always busy—and frequently moved to newer, even more challenging projects. He did that with women too, didn't he? She had to try to remember that.

'Did you know Jayne McIntosh is trying to sell,' Rob said. 'I bet her father regrets not backing you now.'

'Would you be interested in Jayne's property, Lorenzo?' Charlotte asked quietly.

Was it Sophy or had he gone a bit stiff? Who was the Jayne? Was this the McIntosh he'd worked for? He reached for his wine and took a small sip. 'No. I don't think so. We have enough for the label and I'm diversifying elsewhere.'

'He was stupid not to come in at the time.' That was Rob again.

'He was doing what he thought best.' Lorenzo shrugged.

'He made a mistake,' Charlotte muttered.

'No.' Lorenzo's face went blank. 'He did me a favour. He made me want to fight even harder.'

'You were already fighting hard enough,' said Charlotte.

Lorenzo just laughed and put his hand on the older woman's arm.

The rental car was roomy and sleek and, even though it was only a ten-minute drive, she was asleep by the time he parked the car. He switched the engine off and just looked at her in the dim light from the moon and stars. Her hair was amazing. He'd been with her every moment—she hadn't nipped into a salon to have it styled in the two minutes he'd had his back turned. She hadn't even used a hairdryer. But it was in that old Hollywood movie star style again—a straight bob at the top ending in curls at her shoulders. She'd run a comb quickly through it, made sure the part was straight and put a clip in. That was it. Utterly effortless perfection.

That was her all over. But she didn't seem to know it. Always she strived to be more—to be and do everything for everyone. She should just chill out and believe in herself more. Because she was gorgeous—inside and out.

He went round to her side of the car, opened her door and roused her gently.

'Oh, sorry.' Her eyes were slumberous, deep blue.

He held her hand tightly and guided her into the lodge. She blinked as he put the lights on.

'You have been working hard,' he said looking at the table. It was covered. But it was the one lying on the small mirror that caught his attention. The blue was the exact colour of her eyes.

'Put it on for me,' he said, his voice woefully husky.

'It's only dress jewellery.' She played it down as she put it on. 'It's hardly diamonds or pearls.'

'It doesn't need to be. It's beautiful. You're really talented.' He'd known that. It was some of what had driven him to offer her the room, to bring her down here.

But it wasn't the only reason. There was the totally selfish reason as well—to have her for the weekend, all to himself. With no one else making demands on her, no interruptions, no brother or sister or mother calling all the time, scheduling errands for her to run. No, she was here for when *he* wanted. And he wanted her all the time.

He took her on the floor then and there. With her naked other than the beautiful necklace—the blue burning into him as he moved closer, closer still. He couldn't resist touching, couldn't stop touching.

He went back to the vineyards early the next day but finished up hours before he ought to. It didn't matter, much of what he needed could be done by phone. It was more just to see the team face to face. But his mind was elsewhere—and his body ached to catch up with it.

Not good. He rebelled against the unfettered need rising inside. Where was his restraint? His self-control was slipping. It was all wrong—he'd worked so long to gain mastery over his emotions. So why wasn't the passion waning? Why was it getting worse?

* * *

'Come for a run.'

Sophy looked up as Lorenzo stalked in. The electricity in the room surged—she wouldn't have been surprised if all the light bulbs had suddenly blown. 'Is exercise your answer to everything?'

'It is if I'm stuck on a problem or angry or something—it works for me.'

And was he stuck on a problem now, or feeling something stronger? 'You get angry a bit, Lorenzo?'

'I used to.'

Maybe he'd had a bit to be angry about. Casually she put down the pliers. 'Tell me about it.'

He looked at her, his eyes like burnt black holes. 'What is there to tell, Sophy? I was my father's punch bag. Eventually I got taken away but went from foster home to foster home. I didn't adjust well.'

She stared, shocked at the sudden revelation, at the painful viciousness underlying the plain statement of facts. Not many people would 'adjust' to that.

He looked uncomfortable, twisting away from her. 'But I'm not like him. I've never hit a woman, Sophy. And I've never hit anyone who wasn't hitting me first.'

He didn't need to tell her that. 'And you don't get angry any more?'

He relaxed a fraction. 'I prefer to get passionate.'

Yeah, he channelled his aggression elsewhere.

'Passionate about exercise,' she teased softly, wanting to lighten his mood. She knew his bio in the company literature was tellingly sparse. Now she saw his work with the Whistle Fund revealed far more. Art camps, for one thing. Sports days. All the work geared to underprivileged, at risk kids. He identified with them. He'd *been* one. 'Did you get into trouble?'

'Totally.'

'What things did you do?'

He didn't answer.

'How bad?'

'A few stupid things.' He was fudging it. 'The school was good.'

'What kind of stupid things?' Sophy leaned towards him. 'Graffiti?'

His grin flashed. 'You figured it out?'

'You have that place totally secure—there are security cameras, you live on site. And that massive piece appears overnight? No way would you have let that happen.'

He shrugged. 'You got me.'

'You're quite good.' He was better than good. 'Spray cans?'

He nodded. 'But I wipe my own slate clean now. And I only decorate my own property.'

'What else?'

He shook his head. 'Nope. If we're doing the twenty questions, then it's your turn to answer.'

She giggled, thrilled inside that he'd opened up just that touch. 'Okay, what do you want to know?'

'Past boyfriends.'

'No. Really?' That was the most pressing thing he wanted to know about her?

'Uh-huh.' His head bobbed, eyes glinting.

'Not a lot to tell. Dated a couple of boys at high school. Only one serious when I was at university.'

'How serious?'

'We got engaged.'

His eyes widened. 'What happened?'

'I changed my mind.'

'You don't strike me as the kind of person to break a promise easily.'

'It wasn't easy. I left the country.'

'Where did you go?'

'France for most of the time.'

'Why did you come back?

'I missed my family.' She shrugged. 'Stupid huh?'

'No. Not stupid.' He went to his pack and pulled out his training gear. 'What did you do at university?'

She'd started law, of course. Had done okay, but didn't have the family brilliance. 'I didn't graduate.'

'Snap. I left to build the business. Why did you quit?'

She swallowed. 'That boyfriend. Bad news.'

'What did he do?'

Cheated, of course. He'd been a law student a few years ahead of her. But he'd only wanted to be with her because of her family's prestige. She didn't want to go there. 'It's more than past your turn for a question. Past girlfriends?'

He bent and tied his trainer laces. 'No relationships Sophy, remember?'

'What about Jayne McIntosh?'

His fingers stilled. 'What did Charlotte tell you?'

Barely anything—it was a guess. So was her next question. 'It wasn't that she didn't turn you on any more, was it?'

He stood. 'I never liked this game.'

'What happened?'

'Nothing that matters,' he said shortly. 'I'm more interested in what's happening now. Not the past, not the future, but now.'

'And what is happening now?' She drew in her lip, wondering if he'd go *there*—dissect their affair at all.

He paused too. Finally turned—away from her. 'We're going for that run.'

They got her some running shoes and shorts from a shop in the town and then he led the way—up the hill, round and down through the forest, finally returning to town and the thermal pools.

Back at the chalet she dressed in his jeans and he cracked the whip.

'You get back to work.'

It was all right for him—he was sprawled on the sofa reading the paper. But she was on target so found going back to work wasn't so hard at all.

A couple of hours later he went out, brought back some Thai takeaway for dinner. After they'd eaten Sophy felt as playful as a kitten—the happiness made her feel sparkly from the inside out. She'd had a wonderful afternoon, was pleased with her progress for the show, and had loved his quiet company. She stood up from the sofa, stretched her arms out and twirled round the room.

'What are you doing?'

'Expressing myself.' She lifted her tee shirt and his smile widened. Oh, it was so easy to have fun with him. 'Come into the bedroom and watch me express myself some more,' she invited.

She danced the way through, peeling the tee shirt from her body. He followed, and she pushed him onto the bed and knelt over him, enjoying the dominant position. Well, she was wearing his trousers, so she'd be in charge. She knew he liked it slow, and she could do slow for him. She toyed with the edges of her bikini top. He reached out and teased one triangle down a little lower so her nipple was almost exposed.

She slapped his hand away from her. 'No. My job.'

His mouth made an 'oh' and his grin went wider. And thirty seconds later his fingers were back teasing—ruining her concentration.

'Stop it.' She batted his hand away again.

'Make me.'

She paused, an idea bolting in. 'Okay.'

She got off the bed and went out to the table covered in all her supplies. The ribbon was scarlet, a thin smooth satin. She picked up some scissors too.

He saw them as soon as she went back into the bedroom. Guessed her intention immediately. 'Oh, no.'

'Hands up.'

'No.'

'Why, Lorenzo—' she knelt on the bed '—you wouldn't be afraid, would you?'

He gave her a piercing look and held out his hands with a pained sigh. 'There was me thinking you were straight-laced.'

'Maybe I've discovered a ribbon of recklessness,' she joked. It was his fault. His influence. His touch. He made her feel free. He made her feel as if she could do anything, try anything, and he'd still accept her.

She bound his wrists together. Wrapped the ribbon around the headboard and tied that too, so his arms were caught above his head. She looked down at his face. He had a smirk. As soon as she finished, he flexed, the ribbon went taut.

His smirk vanished. He stiffened and pulled harder.

'I don't think you can break it.' She leaned closer to him, letting her breasts touch as she taunted. 'We girl scouts know how to tie knots.'

He pulled again. She saw it dawn in his eyes—that he really couldn't get free. 'Sophy. Untie them.'

'No.' She straddled him.

'Sophy. Joke's over.' He looked very serious, his eyes black.

'It's no joke. And it's not over.' She tickled her fingers up the underside of his arms—his biceps bulging as he tried to rip free of the ribbon again. 'Don't worry,' she whispered. 'I won't hurt you.'

The tenor had changed completely—he really wasn't comfortable with this, was he? She studied him. Raw, vulnerable, yet fiercely proud. Something pulled deep in her heart. This powerful, independent man was at her mercy—and he didn't like it.

And what had begun as an almost kinky, definitely playful tease, turned devastatingly intense. She spread her fingers wide, ran her palm slowly up the centre of his chest, feeling the warm skin, up to where she could feel the thudding of his heart. Had he ever lain back and just let someone *love* him?

No. He never had. And he didn't want to let her now.

But she wanted to love him—so much. And just this once, she would.

She moved off him, knelt at his side and started—slowly—even more slowly than when he'd tormented her that first time. She touched him, forgot time as she felt him, entranced in her exploration in seeing how she could make him respond. Making love to every inch of his skin and trying to go deeper—right into his bones, into his heart. He said nothing. Nor did she. But his breathing changed. She watched the straining in his body—knew what he wanted. She was breathless too—filled with yearning. She kissed him all over, her fingers either trailing or kneading every part of him—but the most obvious. She was saving the best bits 'til last. It was too wonderful to rush it.

But eventually she moved closer—her hands working together in sweeping circles—ever decreasing—narrowing in on her target. She heard his breath catch.

'Sophy.'

She smiled and took him in her mouth. His harsh groan

was the sweetest melody to her ears. He moved beneath her—arching, seeking.

'I want to touch you,' he ground out, his hips rising—chasing her caresses.

'You already are.' It was her turn to be fiercely proud—of the way she could make his powerful body buck, of the way she could make him cry out for her. The pleasure she could give him. She wanted to make him feel joy—as being with him filled her with joy. And the feelings surged through her, she lifted up looked down into his eyes. The beautiful eyes that she loved.

She kissed him like crazy—pouring it all into him. He met her, his kiss equally fervent. Then his body went rigid beneath her as he strained to be free of the bonds, but the knots held.

'I have to have you.' He sounded so raw. 'Please.'

Finally she couldn't take it any more herself—needed to feel him deep within her. She straddled him. Held his pulsing erection in her hand and sank onto him in one swift movement. They both cried out. He arched up, trying to lead the rhythm, but she pushed her hands down on his shoulders, using them as anchors so she could ride him hard—her way. She threw her head back as the bliss ravaged through her.

'Sophy, Sophy, Sophy.'

She looked back down into his eyes as she heard his agonised call to her. Saw him stripped bare. The vulnerability unconcealed—the bottomless depth of need in him revealed. Her fingers tightened on him as she saw the anguish there. She leaned forward to kiss him again—a kiss offering all she had. And felt the shudders racking him as he accepted it.

A long time later she still lay on him, running her hand gently over his chest as she felt his heartbeat slow. She said nothing, didn't expect him to either—and he didn't. Eventually she moved, lifting to look at him. His eyes were closed, his brow smooth. She pulled the coverings up. He'd gone to sleep. She reached down to the floor and got the scissors. She caressed his jaw, pressing a soft kiss to his cheek. And then she snipped the ribbon.

He moved faster than she'd ever have thought possible. Grasping both her hands in his, he flipped her onto her back, his eyes open and blazing as he crushed her half beneath his body. The scissors clattered to the floor. Breathless, she twisted her head to the side—could see the red marks on his wrists from where he'd fought against the knots. She bit her lip, braced as she looked back into his face—afraid of the anger she would find there.

But the flames weren't frightening. Instead the faintest smile appeared as he pushed down to emphasise each word. 'No one. But. You.'

CHAPTER NINE

LORENZO could hear Sophy playing with the necklace—picking it up, rolling the beads between her fingers, letting it drop. And then picking it up again. He kept his gaze on the dark grey bitumen that was fast sliding under the car. The airport was a rush of bodies and noise and interminable waiting—even though they arrived only five minutes before the check-in for their flight closed. Too soon they landed in Auckland. Too soon he was driving her home.

And he was not going in with her.

'Are you pleased with your designs?'

She nodded, dropping the necklace against her skin once more.

'I'll take them back to the warehouse. You can do any finishing there this week.' He couldn't bring himself to sever it completely. Not yet.

'Thanks.' She didn't look him in the eye. And he didn't look for long to see if she did.

Breathing space. He couldn't wait to be alone so he could reclaim his equilibrium. Alone was good. Alone was comfortable—this wasn't. The discomfort was bigger than the silence that ballooned between them.

He reached into his pocket and pulled out her phone. The shock on her face sent a welcome flash of pleasure through him. Yeah, she'd forgotten he had it. She'd forgotten everything else the whole weekend except her work. And him.

That pleased him far too much, and in the wake of the warm glow the discomfort barged back.

'See you tomorrow, Sophy.' He drove away as soon as she was out of the car.

Something had changed. He knew when it had, but he wasn't sure how. She'd held him and he'd been more vulnerable than ever before in his life. But it wasn't because she'd bound his hands.

He didn't care to think about what had happened—what he might have revealed or what she thought she might have seen. But the need to have more of what she'd given had driven him. Just for today he'd taken it—holding her, playing with her, laughing like the carefree kid he'd never been. She'd done some work—not that much—they'd swum, they'd rested. A lovely, lazy Sunday for anyone normal.

But he wasn't normal—was fundamentally different from most and especially someone like Sophy with her perfect world and her perfect family. And now—back on normal ground—he was feeling more alien than ever.

Restless in his apartment, he tried to catch up on some work—went through the motions of checking his messages. He felt as if he'd stolen someone else's life for a day and he was going to get caught out any moment. His heart pounded the way it had when he was a kid and had known trouble was coming. His concentration splintered, reformed—focused on only one thing.

He went down to the room she'd taken as a workshop. Went into the cupboard at the back and pulled out the crate of paint. Twelve hours later he was still working on it in his office, hating the way he was so wired about seeing her.

'Stay late tonight—I've got something to show you.' He poked his head into her office halfway through the next day, not staying to explain, glad she had the temp with her so he couldn't go and kiss the hell out of her as he wanted. He was a touch embarrassed. She might not like what he'd done. And wasn't he just getting himself in an even stickier mess? He should be pulling away, not going in deeper.

Lorenzo was no stranger to hardship—well used to going without. So a bit of abstinence should be nothing. But she was the first thing—the only thing—that he wasn't sure he could give up.

He'd noticed she was missing something for the show and he was certain she hadn't had time to do it herself. She was up to her neck just trying to get the pieces done. She came to his office on the dot of five. He'd abandoned work hours ago—had been shooting hoops half the afternoon, was now sitting waiting.

'It's upstairs.' He almost blushed. But the screen of his computer up there was bigger—that was why—not because up there was private and had his huge bed waiting. She said nothing, just followed. He swung the computer screen round so she could see. 'I did some designs for you. If you want to use any I can get them printed.'

She stopped in front of the computer and stared at the images he'd pulled up. 'For business cards?'

He nodded. 'And labels for each piece—you can write on the details by hand or do them on the computer individually.'

Her eyes were wide as she bent to take a closer look. 'You're a man of many talents, aren't you?'

'Some good, some not so good.'

'Lorenzo, they're amazing.' She looked so thrilled he was even more embarrassed. 'I can't believe you did this for me.'

He shifted uncomfortably. 'It didn't take anything. It's really easy.' Okay, it hadn't been that easy. He'd stayed up half the night painting and then spent half the morning getting them into digital form. And then playing some more with them.

'I won't mind if you don't want to use them.'

'Of course I want to.' She was already fiddling with the mouse, tapping words. 'Lorenzo, this is fantastic. Thank you so much—I love them.'

'Okay.' He felt the relief whistle through him. 'Well, you want to work on them now? Then I'll get them printed. You'll be right on schedule.'

He went to the coffee machine. Hadn't slept all night, didn't need the hit now, but it was something to do. He glanced over to his workspace—she'd pulled up the seat and was busy adjusting his designs, experimenting with the text to go across the swirling design he'd created as her logo.

His heart thudded even more uncomfortably as the edge of panic sliced into him. He glanced at the door. This wasn't just his place, but his *escape*—his private lair. So why the hell had he tainted it with her scent again? It had taken days to fade after the last time she'd been here—when he'd been stupidly sick. And her scent had tormented his fever then. It was swirling round him now—tempting, choking him.

He shouldn't feel annoyed she was here—he'd invited her, after all. But now he wished he hadn't. He needed to get out before he did something stupid. All he could see was the memory of her lush mouth sucking him in, the look in her eyes as she'd arched above him.

'Um…' he walked away '…I'm going for a run.'

She looked up from the computer. 'Now?'

'Uh-huh.' He moved as fast as possible. If he didn't the concrete would set around him and he'd be stuck completely.

As soon as he changed into shorts and trainers he got

out onto the pavement and pushed it from the off. But with every pound of his feet the pull sharpened. It was like being torn in two. He pushed harder. Aimed to go further. But... he couldn't fight it. Any hope of restraint faded. He turned back.

The door slammed behind him. His breathlessness didn't ease. His erection grew harder. He'd run from her yet in less than twenty minutes was running back to her faster than before. His fingers curled tighter in his fists. She looked up as he strode across the room. He winced as her cool gaze swept over him. No way could she fail to see the state he was in. He walked across the room.

'You're going to shower?'

He nodded and strode faster. The torment infuriated him. He faced the shower head, turning the jet onto full power. Not caring that the gush of water was slightly too hot and needling his nipples. His sensitive nipples. He'd managed to go without all kinds of things before—why not now? He braced his hands on the wall and pushed his face into the rush of water, wanting to wash away the desire he felt for her. Wanting the emptiness back. It was easier—so much easier.

A hand slipped around his body. He gasped as she grasped his straining erection. He could feel her soft body against his back. And then her other arm wrapped round him too, her fingers teasing circles around one of those too sensitive nipples—tormenting him further. 'Sophy, don't.' The words hurt. Everything hurt.

'Do you really mean that?'

'You don't know what will happen.'

Her mouth moved across the skin stretching across his tense shoulders. 'Don't I?'

He pushed harder against the wall with his hands, desperate to thrust his hips. This would all be over in a second if he didn't get a grip. But it was her grip that tightened—pulling up his length with faster, harder strokes.

'Sophy.' He whirled around and pulled her close.

She shivered as he brushed his lips up the length of her neck in the gentlest ever touch—the sweeping caress a complete contrast to the rough, hard hold of his hands. He struggled to soften that hold—but couldn't, so made his kisses light instead.

'I want you so bad,' he confessed.

'That's not a bad thing.'

Oh, but it was. The water thundered in his ears. She was so soft—so heart-meltingly soft. But it was because she was so soft that he should be staying away. Instead he leaned into her, his lips trailing over her jaw, sucking her lip. He felt the insane need to touch strengthen again. His need to be with her was unstoppable now.

'Are you too sore?' He tried to slow down—they had been so physical yesterday and he was sure she must be tender.

'No.'

'Are you sure?'

She arched, lifted her legs to curl them around his thighs—opening to give him all access. And as he felt the wet heart of her sliding against him he lost it. Couldn't stop now even if he tried, the last shred of control gone. His hands moved, fingers gripping tight, holding her so she couldn't move.

He was hardly conscious of her cries as he mindlessly pumped deeper and deeper, growling as he strove for the bliss only a stroke or two away.

Instinctive, elemental, shattering—*peace*.

For a long moment he remained still, rammed into her body, trying to stop his weak shuddering in the aftermath. The hot water cascaded over him but inside the chill was spreading fast and painfully. So out of control. He'd been so hopelessly out of control. He didn't even know if—

Oh, God, what had he done?

'Better now?' She ran her hand lightly down the side of his neck.

He screwed his eyes shut, wanting to reject her touch.

Because, no, he was *not* better. His body might be spent, but he still wasn't satisfied. He didn't know if he ever would be. The feelings scared him. He couldn't suppress them. It had never happened before. Never been like this. 'I'm sorry.' He shook his head and made himself look at her. 'You didn't have time.' Hell—had he hurt her?

'Didn't I?'

He saw a smile stretch her puffy lips, the pure satisfaction glowing from inside out. 'Really?' But it didn't ease his conscience.

She closed her eyes, tilted her head to let the water flow over her face.

Her beauty hurt him. Everything about her hurt him.

Because he could have hurt her. He wouldn't even have known—certainly wouldn't have been able to stop. In those moments just now, he'd totally lost it. The wild animal he knew was caged inside him had been freed—he'd been operating on blind, raw emotion and been utterly unable to think, to be aware of anything but his need to let that emotion have free rein. Just as he had all those years ago. Only then he'd pulverised some random person's car—had taken a bat to it in a blind rage, had smashed and destroyed, his anger thermonuclear. Unstoppable. Uncontrollable. Terrifying.

Loss of control over his emotions was unacceptable. It didn't matter what emotion—lust was as bad as anger. And if he'd lost it over one, he could lose it over another just as easily. The years of hard work, the self-discipline gained from physical training and concentration meant nothing now. He'd thought he could manage it? He didn't have a hope.

And hurting anyone—hurting *her*—was not an option. He'd always choose isolation over running that risk. And he'd enforce it now.

He looked at her—she wasn't even naked. She'd only stopped to take off her knickers before reaching to touch him as he'd showered. And now she was wet and bedraggled and beautiful.

Her eyes opened and in that moment he saw it—the vulnerability, the confusion, the *questions*. His blood ran cold. He couldn't possibly answer those questions.

He pushed away, switched the water off and got out of the intimacy of the shower room. 'Here.' He handed her a towel. 'Strip off and I'll hang your clothes to dry.'

They needed to talk. It was a talk they should have had the day before but she'd been too scared. Honestly she was still too scared. She didn't want to shatter this fragile moment—this happiness seemed so fleeting.

But it was disappearing anyway. She could see him retreating. His face had frozen, the brooding look back in his eyes. She tried not to let it hurt her. But that was like trying to stop the sun from rising.

'Don't worry,' she said, suddenly realising what might be bothering him. 'I've started the pill. I won't get pregnant.'

'What?' He spun to face her.

She blinked. 'In the shower just now, we ah…' She didn't finish.

His eyes had widened in horror. 'You've started taking the pill?'

'I thought it was for the best.' She didn't want babies

yet. Judging by the look on his face he didn't want babies at all. So it was better not to run the risk of accidents. She'd known it was the wise thing to do.

'When?'

When had she started taking it? 'Last week.'

'Oh.' He still looked shocked, only now a frown had overlaid the discomfort on his features too. 'I'll, um…just find you a robe.'

He hurried from the bathroom.

An affair. She rubbed her skin hard with a towel and tried to remind herself that that was all it was. A one night fling that was having a few replays—okay, was on a continuous loop. But she couldn't make herself believe that was all there was to it despite his rapid cooling off now. If she were sensible, if she were reading the signs, she'd stop it. Walk away. But she was utterly lost in the web of desire for him. Her body held in thrall by his. And there was more than that.

She was in love with him. Head first, totally, desperately in love with this complicated, lonely, generous man. She ached to give him everything—and could only hope that maybe he'd ask for it, maybe accept it. She couldn't end it now—it would be like ripping out her own heart.

She walked back to the living area, looked at the cards he'd designed on the computer. He'd clearly studied her work—because he'd done the samples in her favourite colours, the swirling design that she saw was a key part of her style. He really did have an eye. The fact he'd done them for her blew her away—and gave her hope. Then she turned and looked at the way he was frowning into the fridge, seeming to take hours to decide what he was looking for.

Suddenly she knew what she had to do—there was even a song about it, wasn't there? About setting something you loved free. 'You know, I can get my clothes tomorrow. If you wouldn't mind me borrowing your robe and you running me home?'

He looked up quickly. 'You don't want to stay?'

Of course she did. But his relief was heartbreakingly obvious.

'No.' She pulled the robe closer around her. It was a warm day but she was growing colder by the second. He didn't want her to stay. Her heart shrank from the truth. She didn't want to be where she wasn't really wanted. He'd just had all he wanted.

Stupid girl.

She stayed away from work the next day—phoned through to Jemma the temp and explained she had family stuff to tend to. Not an untruth. She always had family stuff to tend to. Lorenzo didn't call, didn't come to her flat that night. She pretended to sleep. He'd never called her phone before—there was no need to be checking it every three minutes all night.

On Wednesday she went in—had to finish up the last details and pack everything up to take it to the theatre. She checked with Kat on the way in, hoped she hid her disappointment when the receptionist told her Lorenzo was scheduled to be out at meetings most of the day. It was a good thing really—she still had a few hours' work to do. She didn't need the distraction.

She worked hard—the labels and business cards were printed and in a box waiting on the table. She was thrilled with the finished product, for the first time feeling excitement about the show. She'd done her best work and now she was excited about showing it to the world. Late in the day she heard the heavy tread on the stairs, couldn't stop from flying to the doorway with an all over body smile that was impossible to hold back.

'Why are you looking so happy?' The brooding shadows were dark beneath his eyes.

Some instinct warned her not to admit that it was because he'd just appeared. 'I've found the most fabulous frock to wear tomorrow night.'

The smallest of smiles lifted his expression and he came into the room. 'Of course. Shopping maketh a woman smile.'

Oh, no, in truth it was just him. 'I'm actually starting to look forward to it now.' And she was. Sure, she was nervous about what her family would think of her designs, but at least she did have a stellar outfit to go in—and an even better escort. 'Are you wearing a tux? It's formal dress.'

His eyes narrowed a fraction and he turned away. 'I'm not going.'

She looked after him, stunned. 'Not going? You're not coming to the opening?'

He walked over to the window. 'No. We're not a couple, Sophy. I said from the start that this wasn't ever going to be a public thing.'

What? But he was the one who'd taken her out to dine with some of his oldest colleagues last weekend. She tried to stay cool. 'Well, you don't have to be there with your arm around me. You could just be there as a friend.'

'You don't need me there.'

'Yes, I do.' She didn't want to go without a friend. Rosanna was away on another buying trip so she wouldn't be there. But that was beside the point—she wanted Lorenzo with her, even just his presence on the far side of the room would be calming—like a secret injection of confidence. He believed in her, she knew he did. And she drew strength from it.

'No. You don't.'

She'd have to face her family's judgment alone. She

swallowed. Okay, she could handle those nerves. But she was hurt by him now. 'Why don't you want to be there?'

'I don't like those foreign type movies.' He shrugged.

'Then why do you have some in your DVD collection?'

'You went through my collection?'

'You know I did.'

'Look, Sophy—' he turned to face her '—leave it. I'm not going.'

'You really don't want to be seen with me?'

'I'm not interested in complicating our arrangement.'

Their *arrangement*? What the hell did he mean by that? 'Then why have you been helping me so much if you're not interested? You want me to do well—why don't you want to be there to see if it happens?'

He turned, irritable. 'It's just sex between us, Sophy— some down and dirty release. It's what you wanted, remember? You can't go changing it now.'

'I'm not.' Her voice rose. 'You've *already* changed it. You were the one who took me away for the weekend. You're the one doing these things for me.'

'That was just so you could get your work done. You were so busy doing everything for everyone else. I thought it was a good way for you to catch up.'

'And that's not showing you care about me—not even just a little?' She held her breath.

He went utterly still. 'Nothing special, Sophy, no.'

She flinched but forced herself to take a step closer. 'And there was nothing in that weekend for you? Nothing *special*?'

He stared at the floor, answered with inhuman control. 'No.' He lifted his head sharply, like a beast sensing blood. 'Now don't get upset.'

'How can I not when you say there's nothing special?'

He was denying everything—denying her, denying himself and above all denying the truth. She couldn't stop the hurt brimming in her eyes as she cried, 'You're lying to me, Lorenzo. And you're lying to yourself.'

'No. I'm being honest.'

She clutched the back of a chair. Was he? Being brutal to be kind? She stared at his rigid body, his masklike face. 'I don't believe you are.'

'It's just sex, Sophy.' His mouth moved, but his eyes were like dull stones. 'Just a tawdry affair that no one need ever know about.'

'You really think that?'

'We have nothing in common. We're good at screwing, that's all.'

She blanched at his crudeness. They didn't screw—she didn't just bang him for the momentary thrill. She'd made love to him—again and again. She had offered everything inside herself to him—wordlessly at least, on more than one occasion.

But she wasn't going to offer it again now—not in the face of such determined denial and such cold anger. No—she had very little left in her right now, but she did have that last drop of dignity. 'Then if that's all it is, Lorenzo, you won't mind that it's over.'

She walked past his stock-still figure and straight down the stairs.

CHAPTER TEN

Sophy slowly buttoned the royal blue nineteen-forties vintage frock she'd found in an exclusive retro store earlier in the week. She pushed out the fantasy she'd had about twirling in it in front of Lorenzo. She spent ages on her face, going with forties style make-up to match—full foundation, lush red lips. She breathed slowly to try to check her nerves.

She'd spent half the afternoon in the theatre foyer setting up the display, had received gratifying comments from the staff there about her designs. But they weren't the people who mattered. She was going to those people now. It was only a ten minute walk to her parents' home in the heart of Auckland; they were going to the theatre together from there.

'I'm looking forward to the movie. It's had great reviews,' her mother chatted, oblivious to Sophy's stress.

Of course, they didn't even realise the exhibition was on in the foyer. Sophy clutched her purse, trying to hide the way her fingers were shaking as her father drove them. Her heart raced. This wasn't good. She'd even done a Lorenzo and gone for a run earlier—too bad if her cheeks were still flushed from it, she'd needed to burn off some of the adrenalin. But she might as well have not bothered. Her body felt wired, on fire, yet she was cold to the bone. She wanted the movie to start—not have a whole hour of the pre-drinks to get through with her stupid baubles on show. But her parents were only too willing to relax, quietly chatting in the foyer to friends and generally acting like the reserved pillars of society that they were. How had she ever thought this was a good idea?

Her brother and sister were already there. And it was her sister and sister-in-law who pointed out the gleaming display cabinets of vintage inspired jewellery to her and her mother.

'What do you think of them?' That was her sister-in-law, Mina.

'I love this one—look at it, Soph, it's just gorgeous,' Victoria said.

'Are you okay, Sophy? You've gone all pale.' Her brother, Ted, stared at her. 'Now you're gone all red.'

'I'm fine,' she squeaked.

Her mother turned to look at her. 'Are you sure?'

'Mmm hmm.' She nodded, not bothering to try to talk more.

'This one would really suit you.' Mina, her sister-in-law, hadn't been paying attention. 'It would go beautifully with your eyes.' She was looking at the blue necklace she'd made in Hanmer.

Ted, her brother—the one with the IQ too high for anyone's good—had picked up one of the business cards on the table.

'"Designs by Sophy,"' he read aloud. 'Even has your mobile number listed.' He gave her a sharp look. 'Got something to share, baby sis?'

'*You* made these?' Her mother whirled, her face beaming.

They all turned and looked at her.

'Umm.' Sophy was a dehydrated flower withering under the heat of her immediate family's collective stare. 'Yes.'

'But this is amazing! Edward!' Her mother raised her voice. 'Edward have you seen these?'

He had—her father put his arm around her, smiling in that quietly pleased way he had. 'Well done, Sophy.'

'You're *so* talented.'

'When did you learn to do this?'

'I could never do anything so intricate.'

Victoria and Mina got in on the act. Oh, the squeals were embarrassing.

'She got it from my side of the family,' her father said with his usual assured authority. 'Which is your favourite, darling?' He turned to her mother. 'I'm going to buy it.'

'You don't have to do that, Dad,' Sophy mumbled, beyond embarrassed by their effusiveness now.

'Oh I do. I am.' He was halfway through the crowds— off to find the manager who was in charge of the sales.

Sophy looked at them. It was weird how her heart could sink and lift at the same time. Wasn't this what she'd wanted? To have their approval? To 'wow' them like this? So why was she feeling so deflated? 'Guys, you don't have to.'

And she realised the problem. It wasn't them she'd wanted to impress. She wanted Lorenzo with her—here to witness it, here to stand beside her. She'd be so proud then.

Her anger flared within—with herself. She'd spent so long wanting this moment—for her parents to be proud of her. How could she let a guy, especially one whom she'd known for all of three weeks, ruin it all? Why was what he thought suddenly so much more important than everything else?

She made herself smile. 'I'm really glad you like them.'

'Like them?' Her mother looked stunned. 'Sophy, we had no idea.'

Sophy shrugged her shoulders. 'You've been busy. I've been busy too—I did it in my own time.'

'Why didn't you tell us you were displaying them tonight?'

'I wanted an honest reaction.'

Her sister frowned. 'You were that insecure?'

'Yes,' she admitted. 'I guess I was. Still am.'

'Oh, Sophy,' her mother scolded but folded her into a hug at the same time.

Sophy smiled. They did look good. The jewellery gleamed in the cases, the display was slick, professional and *different*—vintage inspired but thoroughly modern.

'Darling, I can't buy that necklace.' Her father came back.

Sophy looked up.

'It's already sold.' He was beaming now. It was just like the smile he'd worn when Ted and Victoria had both graduated with their first class law degrees, the smile she'd never seen him bestow on her before. 'Apparently it was the first item that went. Several of the other pieces have sold now too. It's a huge success, Sophy.'

Sophy flushed with pleasure.

'Apparently it sold within five minutes of them opening the doors tonight. Someone was obviously keen.'

Sophy's flush deepened. Her thoughts instantly flicked to Lorenzo—had he done it? Was he here for her as a surprise? Had he bought the necklace because of what they'd shared? Was this his way of apologising?

Her heart soared with hope.

'Sophy, there's someone here wanting to talk to you.' Her brother touched her shoulder.

Sophy spun, blood thundering in her ears as she looked

through the crowds. He was here—he'd come. Someone tapped her other shoulder and she turned again, getting hopelessly giddy, and too full of hope.

'Surprise!'

'Oh!' Sophy gasped. 'Rosanna!' She threw her arms around her friend and hugged her close—hiding her disappointment in her friend's shoulder and her tight hug.

'You didn't think I'd really miss it did you?'

Sophy shook her head. She couldn't speak, her heart full and yet bleeding at the same time. She had such a great friend, such a great family. She had no right to be feeling so crushed. She looked into her friend's smiling face. 'Oh, thank you so much for coming.'

Lorenzo sat in his car, still too shocked to even turn the key. He was parked just down the road from the theatre—had been since ten minutes before the doors opened and that was an hour ago now. Fool that he was, he hadn't been able to resist.

He'd been going to go—say sorry, or something. He hadn't meant a word of what he'd said yesterday. He'd done it deliberately—pushed at her until she pushed him away. But she was right, he'd been lying. Of course she was special. She was so special he was terrified.

So here he was sitting in his damn monkey suit and everything because he couldn't let her down completely. But thank goodness he had. Because now he knew.

Braithwaite. It wasn't that common a surname. He should have made the connection sooner. But he hadn't bothered to ask too much. And she offered almost as little info about her family as he did his. Now he knew why.

The collar of his shirt seemed to be tightening round his neck—choking him.

He'd seen them arrive before he'd got out and got in

there. For once the fates had shown him some mercy. Because the last thing he'd have wanted was to have met the man again in front of Sophy.

Edward Braithwaite—*Judge* Braithwaite—the man he'd stood before all those years ago. The one who'd condemned him and yet who had offered him that one last chance.

For half an hour tonight, while dressing, he'd deluded himself into thinking he could have fudged it—hadn't enough time passed? Jayne's father had sent him packing— he wasn't good enough for his daughter, wasn't good enough to invest in back then. And she'd agreed—had laughed at his dreams. He'd just been sex to her.

But ten years had passed since then and things had changed. Some things anyway. So maybe, if it was someone else, he could have pulled it off—skirted round his history and talked up his present successes. But Judge Braithwaite knew everything—had seen him at his worst. He knew the whole sorry story. And no way would he want him anywhere near his precious baby daughter.

Society might give second chances, fathers didn't. Fathers wanted only the best for their daughters; hell, Lorenzo understood that—*he* wanted only what was best for Sophy. And that wasn't him.

He bowed his head over the steering wheel and faced it: it was always going to be this way—as it had been before, it would be again. And it was why he should never have let her get so near to him. The past was inescapable. The perfect life he'd been imagining for just a few moments was a mirage—something that he just wasn't meant to have. He'd managed his life fine without until now anyway—forging his career, working so hard. He had his hugely successful business, the charity, he had a couple of good friends. But any other intimacy? A woman, a life partner—there could be none.

He would never be good enough for a woman as wonderful as Sophy and he wanted none but her. It didn't matter how much money he made, how successful his business became, there was always that part of him—that fundamental truth that he always tried to hide even from himself.

But her father knew that truth, and, knowing how much her parents' approval mattered to Sophy, Lorenzo knew it was over.

She deserved a perfect family, a perfect lover. But it would never be him. He had never been part of a family. Had never been wanted in a family. Damn well didn't want one of his own. Being alone was what he was used to—secure, uncomplicated. And he had been a fool to think he could ever deal with anything more—or be dealt anything more.

He had to stay away now. He'd let the end he'd engineered her to declare truly be the end. So there was only one thing left for him to do. He'd go to Vance's bar. And he'd get really, really drunk.

Sophy didn't remember a thing about the movie that screened. Afterwards she went with her family for coffee and cake—Rosanna came too. But all she could think of was the necklace that had sold so quickly. She knew it was crazy, that she'd read too many romance novels and watched too many Hollywood movies, but she couldn't help hoping that he'd bought it for her. Maybe he'd sent someone in to buy the necklace. Maybe he'd present it to her in a romantic gesture, an apology for not being there. It was going to be his way of making it up to her. Oh, how she'd love something like that—for someone to go over the top for her, someone going to lengths to do something wonderful for her.

She was such a sad unit.

'Are you okay?' Rosanna curled her legs up on the café's sofa after Sophy's parents and siblings had called it a night.

Sophy nodded and flopped back into the big armchair. 'I'm just a bit tired.'

Rosanna reached forward and put her glass on the table carefully. 'Lorenzo wasn't there.'

'No. He said he wouldn't be.'

Rosanna's eyes had narrowed. 'But—'

'My mother loved those earrings. Did you see her?' Sophy interrupted. 'I never thought she'd be into ones that are so dangly.'

'I know.' Rosanna went along with the change of topic. 'So are we going out to party now?'

Sophy laughed and shook her head. It was after one a.m. already. 'I don't think so.'

Rosanna shrugged. 'I can come home if you want.'

'And eat chocolate ice cream? No, I'm going straight to bed.'

'Okay. But if you wanted to do the ice cream, you know I'd ditch the plans.' She paused. 'I'm going to meet up with Vance.'

'What about Emmet? And Jay?'

'Oh, they're going to the bar too.'

It was the most genuine laugh to burst from Sophy in days.

Rosanna's face lit up. 'I have a surprise for you—close your eyes.'

Sophy obeyed, waited for what felt like ages. 'Are you still there?'

'Yes.' Rosanna chuckled. 'Okay, you can open them now.'

Sophy did—and stared. Rosanna was wearing the necklace—*her* necklace.

'I just loved it.' Rosanna angled her shoulders one way and then the other, showing off the sparking necklace with its looping swirl.

Sophy made herself swallow the disappointment and bring up a smile. 'It suits you.'

'Don't worry about the display.' Rosanna leaned forward. 'I promised I'd bring it back in tomorrow and leave it for the duration of the festival, but I wanted to surprise you tonight.'

And she had.

Sophy gripped her cup closer to her chest. 'You didn't have to buy it. I'd have given it to you.'

Rosanna flashed her huge smile. 'I know, but I didn't want you to. I wanted you to be a success tonight so I bought it straight away. But then so many others sold too— you're a legend!'

Sophy was so disappointed it was embarrassing. She'd really thought it had been him. That it was going to be some grand gesture, to have her unwrap it as part of an apology and declaration—of what? His *love*?

As if.

Hot tears prickled her eyes.

'Sophy!' Rosanna looked horrified. 'I've made you cry.'

'It's okay.' She tried to pull it together, but the salty water trickled down her cheeks. Yeah, she had wanted that. It had been the private fantasy that had got her through the last few hours. 'Thanks so much for doing that. It means a lot.'

It hadn't been him, of course it hadn't. She'd been an idiot to think it ever could have been. No, it was her best friend who'd done it for her. She'd been the one to turn up. Sophy knew she should stick to the sisterhood. Men were overrated. 'You know what?' She sniffed and reached for her handbag. 'I *am* going to come out with you tonight.'

She was not going to go home and wallow. She wasn't going to waste one more minute of her life mooning over Lorenzo. She had too much to celebrate tonight. She was going to go dancing.

The bar was pumping. Sophy followed Rosanna to the dance floor. Rosanna had sent a text ahead and Emmett and Jay were waiting with drinks for them.

'Thank you, darlings.' Rosanna kissed them both.

Sophy managed a smile and downed half her glass's contents in one shot.

Jay's brows lifted and he took her arm. 'Come on, you look like you need a laugh.'

Oh, she did. Jay was a great dancer—held her close, had slick moves and didn't once make her feel as if she was his second choice partner—though she knew full well she was. She felt her body relaxing into the relentless beat—it blocked all thought from her head and dulled the pain. Yeah, this had been a great idea. She'd dance 'til dawn and then maybe she'd be able to sleep. She stood on tiptoes so he had a chance of hearing her. 'Thanks, Jay. I'll put in a word for you.'

He slid his hand round her waist and chuckled. 'Every little bit helps. But it's not Emmett I'm worried about. It's the bar dude.' He nodded over to the side.

Sophy turned to look. From behind the bar Vance stood tall, positively glaring over at where the four of them were dancing. She couldn't stop the little laugh. But then it died because someone else stepped up from the back of the bar. Even taller than Vance, Lorenzo was glaring even harder— right at her.

She spun back to face Jay. 'Shall we dance some more?'

'Sure.' He pulled her closer.

But her heart was racing and she could hardly hear the music above the noise in her ears. Only one song later she pushed away. 'I'm just going to freshen up.'

She ran cold water over her hands and wrists, trying to cool down and slow her pulse. Then she got her lipstick out and took care repairing her slightly worn look. Then she simply stared at her reflection and wished she could teleport out of there. She really hadn't liked the look in Lorenzo's eyes.

Finally she left the room. He was leaning against the wall in the corridor, his eyes fixed on the door. She paused—stood back to let another woman past before taking the step clear of the doorway. But she kept her distance from him. Knew getting past him was going to be difficult. He looked like a panther about to pounce.

'You look like you're having a good time,' he drawled.

So did he—his hair was tousled, his eyes burning. He looked as if he'd been propping up the bar for hours.

'I am.' She made herself act perky.

'With one of Rosanna's cast offs,' he muttered.

'He's charming. He's good company. He doesn't take himself too seriously.'

Was that a snort?

She glared at him. 'Why are you so dressed up?' Although the tie was gone it was definitely a tux he was wearing. And even though he wore it carelessly, he wore it too well for her comfort.

He shrugged. 'How did it go?'

'I didn't think you were interested.' She couldn't stop the bitchiness.

He lifted away from the wall. 'Sophy.'

'No.' She straightened, getting ready to move. 'I've got

someone waiting for me.' She moved fast to get past. But he pounced—just as she'd known he would.

Damn, his hands were fast and he was too strong. In seconds he'd pulled her into a room and locked the door. A toilet. Really classy.

But before she could even start in on the fury she felt he'd pulled her close. His hand cupped her chin, tilting her head back for him to kiss.

But he didn't go for her mouth—no, it was her jaw, her neck, that spot beneath her ear that they both knew was so sensitive. She could smell the alcohol on him, could feel how thin his control was and then she felt his lips. That damn sweet tenderness that made her feel as if he was worshipping her with his mouth. She fell back, melting into the kisses; his furious passion rose in a flash, sweeping her away.

It had been three days. Three long, lonely days in which she hadn't felt his touch—and as soon as she did she flamed for him. Despite her hurt and disappointment she still wanted him—desperately.

His kisses deepened as she softened. She panted as he kissed her with ravenous abandon, his hands cupping her butt and rhythmically pressing her against his hard erection as his mouth scalded her skin.

But as his touch grew bolder, more intimate, her brain started screaming at her. He didn't want to go out with her—be seen together by their friends or family. But he'd whisk her into the nearest, tackiest place he could so he could get his hands on her? He was the proverbial dog in the manger. Not wanting her but not wanting her to have fun with anyone else? Not fair. Not right.

She grabbed his chin and forced it up, making him look into her face. Her nails curled into the vulnerable space just below his jawbone. If she were truly part animal she could kill him this way—pierce the skin and slice his throat. But that wouldn't serve her purpose at all. She wouldn't scratch him, couldn't hurt him—not that way at least—despite the anger burning inside her, and the bottomless well of pain that was feeding it.

For a long moment she looked into his eyes—saw her anger reflected. What bothered him so much? Surely not her dancing with Jay?

No, this anger was too deep for that. And too old. It was the bitterness she'd seen in him before, only tonight it was burning out of control.

She looked away, caught sight of their reflection in the mirror—her face pale, her lips that ridiculous bright red from her forties fashion look.

She turned back to him, brushed her lips against his jaw and then looked at his skin. All praise to the modern cosmetics companies with their long-lasting lip colours—but they'd yet to make them smudge free.

She kissed his jaw again, then down his neck, pressing her lips hard all the way down to the starched white collar of his shirt—and then across that. As she made her mark she let her hands tease him, inflame him, distract him.

'Sophy.'

She swore she'd heard that old thread of laughter then—yeah, he was so confident of her surrender. She let her hands slip lower—harder.

She heard his hissing breath, felt the surge of energy and braced herself.

But nothing could prepare her for what happened. His hands twisted in her hair as he held her firm and gazed at her. His burning black eyes bored into hers—but there was no laughter in them, not even a smile. He was all serious, so intense and, if she was right, so sad.

It began as the softest kiss. Then his arms went tight

around her, sealing their length, and she felt him straining against her, his touch scorching, his need overwhelming.

Finally the kiss eased. It was then that she found it—the strength to push him away. To her surprise he let her, his head snapping back as she shoved him hard in the chest.

She blinked away the tears—of bewilderment, resentment and plain old hurt.

'Gosh, Lorenzo—' her voice shook '—you have lipstick stains all over your face and all over your shirt.' Her bitter laugh turned into a sob halfway through. 'How are you going to hide your dirty little secret now?'

The fury that flashed made her run.

'Sophy!'

How she got the door open she never knew. But she ran through the crowded bar, desperate for an escape.

Jay materialised in front of her, eyes wide. 'Sophy?'

Yeah, her little paint job meant she had more than a make-up malfunction now, she probably looked like a reject from clown school with the slut red lipstick smudged all over her chin. 'Walk me to a cab, would you?' She had no idea where Rosanna was but would get Jay to pass the message on later.

'Of course.' He moved instantly.

'I'll do that.' Lorenzo was on the other side of her.

'No, you won't.' She pushed past him.

'Are you okay?' Jay muttered, putting his arm around her, glaring over her head at Lorenzo, who silently stalked next to them.

'Never better. Will you tell Rosanna I've gone home?'

'Sure.'

They got outside. Jay kept a protective arm looped around her shoulders as he stepped to the kerb and waved his spare arm at the taxi rank not far down the road. The first one peeled off and came towards them. Jay stayed with her, holding the door—blocking it from Lorenzo while she got in.

'Sophy.' Deadly quiet but she heard him anyway.

Just before she slammed the door she answered. 'Not now, Lorenzo. I'm too angry, and you're too drunk.'

CHAPTER ELEVEN

SOPHY hadn't been home fifteen minutes when the thudding on her door started.

She opened the door and glared at him. 'I said not now.'

'I'm not drunk.'

'Oh, please.' She looked at the way he was breathing, at the flush in his cheeks. 'Did you run here?'

He shrugged.

'You shouldn't run in those shoes. It'll be bad for your feet.'

'Says the woman wearing stupidly high heels.'

She whirled away and walked down the hall. 'What is it you want, Lorenzo?'

She heard him close the door and walk after her. 'I just wanted you to know it's not you. It's me.'

She stopped and turned back to stare at him. 'You've got to be kidding me.' She laughed. 'That's the line you're giving me?'

'I was jealous as hell watching you dance with him. Even though I knew there was nothing in it, I was wild. I can't even blame the booze. I'm sorry.'

'*You* could have danced with me.'

He shook his head. 'You're too good for me.'

'Oh.' She clasped her hand to her chest. 'Another great

line. Whatever will be next? Let me guess, "I just don't do relationships, darling,"' she said, dropping her voice a ridiculous octave. '"I was born to be alone." Am I on the right path?'

He'd gone pale. Stopped halfway down the hall. 'Why did you want me to meet your family?'

'I didn't. It wasn't like I was going to introduce you to them as my boyfriend or anything, Lorenzo. Heaven forbid.' She rolled her eyes. 'I just wanted you to be there. I wanted your support.'

'No.' Lorenzo took a deep breath in and reminded himself that he was not going to lose it. Not again. Now was the time for some honesty. He owed her that, at least. 'I've met your father before.'

'You have?'

'He was the presiding judge when I was up in court.'

'What?'

'Youth court. I was thirteen.'

'What had you done?'

He shrugged. 'Graffiti, theft, destruction of property. It wasn't the first time.'

'What did he do?'

'Ordered some community service. Made the order to send me to that school.'

'Dad did that?'

'Yes. I had "potential." They thought it might bring it out.' And it had—to a degree.

She lifted her brows. 'And you think what? That your past would put him off you now?'

Of course it would.

'Doesn't all you've done in the last eighteen years count for anything? Or are you stuck in some kind of time warp? You don't think what you've done with your life since matters?'

He shook his head. She just didn't get it.

'So tell me the truth, then.' She squared up to him. 'The wine label—it's a front for money laundering, isn't it?'

'What? No.'

'Is it drugs, then? You're secretly growing pot in the vineyards?'

'Of course not.'

'Oh.' She sounded disappointed. 'No illegal activities. You're not much of a crim then are you?'

'Sophy.' He so didn't need the sarcasm right now.

She didn't stop. 'Have you ever been back in court?'

He shook his head.

'So what's the problem?' She folded her arms and eye-balled him. 'My father believes in justice, Lorenzo. You had a problem. Did some things you shouldn't have. You did your hours of community service or whatever. Put the wrong right. And he got you into a place that would actually help you. It's finished. Behind you.'

'He wouldn't see it like that.'

'How do you know?'

'I just do, all right?' She was so naïve. 'Do you really think he'd be okay with what I'm doing with you?'

'Well—' her colour deepened '—I don't think he'd want to know any intimate kind of details about anyone I'm with but—'

'No father wants a man like me to be with his daughter. No father.'

She lifted her head. 'Someone's said that before?'

'More than once,' he exaggerated. 'Not good enough.'

'You need to lose the chip, Lorenzo,' she said coolly. 'Anyway—' she lifted her head proudly '—I don't live with them. I'm grown up. I make my own choices. I can see whoever I want.'

'You say that but we both know that what your family

thinks means everything to you. You've been tied up in knots for weeks over what they'd think of your work. What they think of your lover would be even worse.' He watched her swallow. Knew he'd scored a hit.

'You're making far too much of something that happened for ever ago. And even if it did bother Dad initially, it wouldn't be a problem once he got to know you now.'

'You just don't get it. I am not the kind of person who should be with you.'

'What kind of person do you think you are? Because I know you. And I know—'

'You don't know me,' he interrupted. 'You've got no idea, Sophy.'

'Tell me, then,' she shouted back.

'Tell you what, Sophy? The ugly truth? How rough it was? How rough I am?'

'Yeah.' Her anger flared. 'Why not tell me some more clichés—the abused-boy stories.'

His vision burst with red. 'What would you know about it? Having to be taken away from your own parents because of the way they treated you? Your father saying you should have been the scum in an abortionist's bucket?'

Sophy recoiled.

'Oh, that was nothing, darling,' he sneered. 'That was just words and not even the worst. Wait 'til you hear the rest.'

'Lorenzo, I'm sor—'

He shouted over her. 'I was beaten for answering him wrong, for not answering soon enough, for not answering at all. It didn't matter what I did, it happened anyway. With fists, sticks, belts—whatever he had to hand. I wasn't wanted by him, wasn't protected by her, and I wasn't wanted by anyone else after. I'd go to a new house, a new home. Meet a new family. Again and again.' He was shaking, bunched his fists to try to stop the uncontrollable jerking of his hands.

'Lorenzo, please—'

His sharp gesture shut her up.

He took a step backwards down the hall, away from her as his agony boiled over. 'You think you can possibly know about it? I sought approval, Sophy. I tried. I would have done anything to make it okay. And I tried everything. But it never worked. It was me that was wrong—every time. So I stopped trying so hard. Because every time it was the same. *Too difficult. Out of control. Angry.* I always stuffed up. Labels stick, so why bother trying? Because in the end you know they don't want you anyway. They never want you.'

'I want you,' she whispered.

It made him incensed. 'No, you don't.'

'I do.' She walked after him.

'You like the sex,' he yelled, taking more steps back. 'This is just an excursion for you. As hard core as you've ever gotten. Your ride with the bad boy. In another week you'll be over it. Go back to someone perfect, Sophy. Someone from the right background, who'll fit into your perfect family.'

'My family aren't perfect.'

He laughed then. 'Oh yeah? Your parents love you. You think they don't but of course they do. They call you all the time, you do things for them all the time. It wouldn't matter what you do, Sophy, no matter how awful, they'll still love you, they'll always love you. But no matter what I did, mine never loved me. And you know the result?' His throat hurt as he hurled the truth out. 'I'm *damaged*, Sophy. Treat someone like an animal and they *become* an animal. And there's no changing that.' That was what her father knew too. 'You have no idea of the rage I can feel. I frighten myself. And I refuse to frighten you.'

He stopped, breathing hard. He couldn't stay in control of anything around her. And it terrified him.

'You don't frighten me, Lorenzo.'

'I can't control it,' he said flatly, admitting the worst. 'I don't want to hurt you.'

'You're hurting me now.'

He shook his head. No, he was protecting her.

'I love you, Lorenzo. Let me love you.'

'No one can love me.' He denied her—he had to. 'And I can't love. I won't.' His back was right up against the door now. 'I can't be part of any kind of family. I tried. And I failed every single time. I won't try again, Sophy. Not even for you.'

'You don't have to. It can just be me, Lorenzo.'

He turned and opened the door. 'It can't,' he said heavily. 'You know it can't. You want it all—and you should have it. The nice guy who loves you, who'll stand at the barbie and talk sport with your father, who'll be a good father to your babies.' He looked over his shoulder at her. 'What the hell kind of dad would I make?' The knife dug deep in his heart and he screwed his eyes tight against the pain. 'I don't need it. Don't want it. Not happening. Not ever happening.' He stood in the open doorway, the cold pre-dawn air chilling the hall. 'I'm sorry I manhandled you tonight. You were right. It's over.'

Sophy cried. Curled into a ball in the hall and sobbed her heart out. So ironic, wasn't it, that the 'perfect' boyfriend had only wanted her for the kudos he could get from her family, while the one she loved wanted nothing to do with her *because* of them—at least in part? After an age she moved, sat staring at the dining table for hours, barely seeing the pattern in the wood as the conversation circled in her head. And her anger with him grew.

Coward. The selfish, bitter coward.

Yet she hurt so much for him—the hell he'd been through. He'd missed out on so much. As a result he didn't understand love. And she wanted to help him understand it. She had to talk to him again, had to show him. Somehow she had to get through to him—or at least try.

By the time she summoned the courage it was after nine the next morning. He was out the back of the warehouse already. He was in jeans, but had no tee on, hadn't shaved. He'd been at it for a while because his body was gleaming. But he didn't stop bouncing the ball. Didn't stop to look at her.

'You're wrong, Lorenzo. You know you're wrong.'

He said nothing.

'You can't stop me loving you.'

He took the shot but missed the hoop.

'You're using it as an excuse. You *like* playing the tortured loner type. It's safe for you. You won't let anyone close because you can't bear to be rejected again. But I wouldn't reject you.'

'You would.' His mouth barely moved.

She stepped in and snatched the ball, forcing him to look at her, to pay attention. 'You're right, my family do love me. No matter what they'll love me. And if they know how happy you make me, they'll love you—regardless of your past. But you won't give them or me a chance because it's easier not to.' She took a shot but missed too. She turned to him as the ball bounced away. 'You're lazy. And you're a coward.'

He looked at her, but there wasn't the fire she'd hoped for. Just the dull stones.

'I can't presume to understand what you went through. I

wouldn't dare to. But I do know this—you can't let it ruin the rest of your life. You can't lose faith in everybody. And I don't believe you have. Why else do you try to help those kids? Why else did you give Vance a chance with the bar? You try to keep yourself shut away but you can't quite do it. And you couldn't do it with me. Only now you're scared. Now you're trying to run. But you don't have to, not from me.'

She stepped closer and took in a deep breath. 'Everyone has problems, Lorenzo. We all do. But problems are best solved with help—and with support from the people who love you.' He didn't have to face his demons alone. She'd stand by his side and help him slay them. As he helped her.

He jerked, looking away from her and going back to the fence to get the ball. She stood, helplessly watching as he started the relentless practising again. She was waiting long moments for what—to be ignored?

She gulped, the burning hurt too strong to be held down any more.

'You know, maybe I do know something of what you went through,' she choked. 'Maybe I do know something about loving someone, of wanting to be loved back but only to be rejected. Not wanted.' The tears suddenly streamed down her face. 'But at the end of the day it's your loss. You could have had everything, Lorenzo. I would have given you *everything*.'

She ran then, wanting to get as far from this hell as she could. Everything—her hope, her heart, her love—was in tatters.

She didn't hear it, didn't see it, as she blindly ran as fast as she could. The last thing she was conscious of was the piercing screech of rubber on metal, and the animal scream in her ears.

CHAPTER TWELVE

THE door opened. Lorenzo turned his head as the woman burst in.

'Where—?' She broke off, gulping as she saw the pale figure in the bed. 'Oh, Sophy.' The tears sprang just like that. 'Is she going to be okay?'

Lorenzo stood but didn't answer and didn't move away. He looked beyond her to the man who'd stopped on the threshold. After a moment that man walked to the other side of the bed and looked down at his daughter for a time, his expression rigid. Then he looked at Lorenzo for even longer, even more frozen.

'I know you.' He didn't smile.

'Yes.' Lorenzo still held her hand. His fingers tightened instinctively. 'I'm not leaving.'

'I can see that.'

'Yeah.' Lorenzo sat down again.

'Beth, this is…' He kept staring at Lorenzo.

'Lorenzo. Lorenzo Hall.'

'That's right.' He nodded slowly. Lorenzo just knew it had all come back to him now.

'Do you know each other?' Her mother looked from her father to him.

Lorenzo looked at the man who had once judged him. Who'd once before given him a chance. And waited.

'Not really.'

Lorenzo looked down at the bed.

'You're a friend of Sophy's?' her mother asked.

'Yes.'

In the silence, nothing more was said.

The guilt was swamping him. It was his fault. If he hadn't made her so upset. If she'd hadn't been at the damn warehouse. If she hadn't run so fast, so blindly from him.

Her blonde hair was spread on the pillow with its perfect curls on the ends. Her skin was unnaturally pale with the ugly bruise deepening. He still couldn't believe there were no broken bones—or worse. He'd waited, utterly distraught, while they'd done their tests. A bad bump to the head, that was all, despite being knocked to the ground, clipped by the edge of the car. It was only the driver's quick action in pulling on the wheel that had saved her from more serious injuries.

The doctors would monitor her for the night, but they didn't think there was anything they'd missed. But even now, despite their words, he feared there was damage beyond what he could see.

'Why don't you call Victoria and Ted, darling?' Sophy's father spoke. 'Go into the lounge area. I'll come and get you if there's any change.'

Lorenzo knew they were communicating behind his back. He didn't care. He wasn't leaving the damn room.

As soon as the door closed behind her he lifted his gaze and met the judge's. He had the same blue eyes as Sophy's—only his were colder. 'Things have changed for you since we last met, Lorenzo.'

'A lot.'

'I'm glad.' He looked serious. 'Does Sophy know?'

'Yes.' Lorenzo swallowed.

'And she's your…friend?'

He knew what he was asking. 'Yes.'

The judge's face tightened. 'You had a lot of potential back then. But when I saw you, you were too angry to use it. Too angry to let anyone care for you. Anyone who tried had it thrown back at them.' His voice changed, to the implacable, imperative word of law. 'Don't you do that to my daughter.'

Lorenzo didn't answer, just looked at the small fingers resting limply in his. He couldn't bring himself to admit that he'd already done exactly that.

Sophy's head really hurt. She blinked. Tried again, squeezing her eyes open just that little bit. 'Lorenzo?'

No answer. But he was here. She was sure of it. She could smell him. She could feel the warmth from the pressure of his hand—he'd been holding it, hadn't he? 'Lorenzo?'

'He's not here,' a deep voice answered. 'I told him to go.'

'What?' she wailed. 'Dad!'

A warm hand touched hers, but it wasn't the right hand.

'Sophy?' Her mother bent over her. 'Honey, are you okay?'

Had she just sobbed? Just a little bit?

'He'll be back. He'll come back, I'm sure. We just told him to go get some coffee. He hadn't moved for almost two hours.'

Okay, so she had sobbed. She closed her eyes again. Felt the wet on her cheek and turned her head away, pressing deeper into the pillow. He wouldn't be back. He didn't want to be near her family—or any family.

'Sophy?'

'Should we get the doctor?' Her mother's voice rose.

'No,' Sophy croaked. 'No. I'm okay.' And with every word she spoke her voice grew stronger. 'What happened?'

'You were hit by a car. You ran straight out onto the road.'

'Were you running away from something, Sophy? Someone?' her father asked quietly, but she heard the tone, the condemnation, the conclusion.

She shook her head, wincing as it hurt. 'Not what you think, Dad.'

'I don't know what to think, sweetheart.'

Carefully she opened her eyes, looked at her father. 'Do you remember him?'

'I remember all of them,' her father said sombrely. 'But some stick in your mind more than others.'

The tears welled again, stinging her eyeballs.

'He was very angry back then. But he had a lot to be angry about.'

Sophy's heart was breaking. She needed her father to know, to understand. 'I love him, Dad.'

The sharp intake of breath was audible—but it didn't come from either of her parents. Sophy turned her head. Lorenzo stood in the doorway.

'You're awake. Are you okay?' The edge of panic was evident both in the speed of the question and the hesitancy as he hovered.

She licked her horribly dry lips.

'Edward, let's go get some fresh coffee.' Her mother suddenly stood. 'Come on. She can't have too many people in here at once. She'll get too tired.'

Sophy watched the two men looking at each other—saw some message she couldn't interpret pass between them.

Lorenzo moved closer, where she could see him better. He was so pale.

'Sophy.' His voice broke. 'I'm so sorry.'

'It was my fault. I should have been watching where I was going.'

He shook his head. 'I shouldn't have made you so upset. I never wanted to hurt you like this.'

The brush-off. Again. It was so embarrassing. Dully she admitted the truth. 'I shouldn't have pushed for something you never wanted to give.'

'You're right,' he said. 'But not about that. I'm scared— just like you said. A coward. You scare me to death—how you make me feel scares me.' He moved quickly, sat in the seat near her head. 'I don't know that I can give you what you want from me.'

'Lorenzo.' She took in a deep breath. She'd take all there was—no matter how little. She loved him. She wanted him. She was happy when with him. She didn't need all the bells and whistles. She just needed him. 'All I want is whatever you have to give.'

He stared at her. The dark eyes tortured, the unhappiness hurting her more than the relentless pounding in her head and in her heart. 'But you deserve so much more than that. So much more than me.'

'No.' Her eyes filled. She didn't want him to push her away like that. No one else could give her what he could. 'I want you. That's all. Just you.'

'And I want you. But I don't want to make you unhappy. And I have.'

She opened her mouth but he kept talking.

'It's all new to me. You know that—the whole big family thing. But I'll try, if you want me to.'

She trembled and his hand quickly covered hers.

'What made you change your mind?'

'Nearly losing you today.' His voice wavered again.

'I got a bump on the head. I'm not about to die—'

'If you had seen yourself you wouldn't say that.'

'Lorenzo, I'm fine.'

'Well, I'm not. I don't think I'll ever recover from seeing you crumple like that.' He closed his eyes and bowed his head, both his hands firmly clasped around hers. 'Can you be patient with me?'

'Yes.' She had him. Nothing else mattered. She didn't need the grand gestures, the romantic flourishes. She just needed him.

He leaned across, kissed her tenderly on the lips. Not enough for her.

'You're staying in here tonight.'

'No.' She frowned. 'I'm not.'

'You are. Observation. You probably have concussion. You need to be monitored.'

'I can be monitored at home. Rosanna will—'

'Rosanna is away,' Lorenzo said sharply. 'I'll wait with you today. Come back to pick you up in the morning. Unless—' he breathed out '—you'd rather your parents did?'

'I want you to.'

His hand cupped her face so gently. 'I don't deserve you.'

'You do,' she said, angry tears springing again. 'You *do.*'

She would make him understand that—somehow. She loved him. But she couldn't say it again—wouldn't—because she didn't want him to feel the pressure to say it in return. She didn't know that he'd ever be able to say it. It didn't matter. Her tortured warrior spoke with actions. And he was here. That was enough.

Twenty-four hours later Lorenzo finally went to do some work for a bit—having instructed her to phone down if she needed anything. He paused halfway down the stairs. Rosanna was on her way up, a sheaf of flowers across one arm.

She waggled her finger at him. 'You don't take my best friend home to your place and think you're not getting me too.'

He laughed. 'She'll be pleased to see you. She's bored and getting restless.'

'I've got some magazines.'

His grin faded as she got closer. 'You're wearing her necklace.' His throat went tight as he saw it.

She touched it. 'Stunning, isn't it? I bought it at the exhibition the other night. Made sure I did it as soon as I got there. I wanted her to have one "sold" sign really early on.' She grinned. 'Not that I needed to worry—she sold most of them in the first hour. But she was so nervous.'

He nodded. 'I know.' He should have thought to do that. That should have been him. But he'd been thinking too selfishly. 'You're a good friend to her.'

'Only because she's wonderful to me. It's nice to be able to do something for her for once,' Rosanna said. 'She does so much for everyone else.'

'Yeah.' She did. She bent over backwards for the ones she loved. She was bending every which way for him. And he wasn't happy about it. She deserved so much more. The feeling inside his chest tightened.

She was going to take him—like this—with nothing extra. She was too generous. And he wasn't going to let her get away with it. Not any more. No matter the cost to him, she was too important. Her happiness was too important.

He could do it, sure he could—because she deserved it.

'I've got a few other things I need to do for her.' He swallowed and bit the bullet. 'Are you up to helping me?'

Rosanna looked sharply curious. 'What kind of things?'

'Top secret things.'

'Spend money kind of top-secret things?'

'Lots of money,' he acknowledged.

'Then you've got an able assistant.'

He'd grin if he weren't feeling so freaked. 'Fantastic.'

CHAPTER THIRTEEN

SOPHY let Lorenzo guide her to her seat. Honestly, she was over the cotton wool treatment. Four days since her accident and he was still handling her as if he was afraid she'd break any moment.

'You're into taking this risk a second time?'

'The first wasn't such a risk,' she teased back. 'It's not like you've asked me for my passport.'

He put his hand in his pocket and pulled out two small blue books.

'No way.' Sophy stared at them. 'You got my passport? How did you do that?'

He didn't answer. Just grinned at her in a lazy way.

'That was at my parents' house.' She frowned. 'At least, I think it was. You didn't break in there, did you?'

'I never did breaking and entering. Not my strength.'

'Don't be ridiculous. You're capable of anything you set your mind to,' she muttered. 'It's scary.'

'Are you scared?'

She met his serious gaze. 'No.' She did up her seat belt. 'Actually I'm hoping you're going to make me a member of the mile high club.'

He laughed but she wasn't kidding. He'd kissed her since the accident, but they hadn't had sex. And she needed it— badly wanted to connect with him. There was a distance between them. She sensed his tension, as if he was keeping something back from her.

'Are we going back to Hanmer?'

He just smiled.

She was sure of it when they got into the rental car in Christchurch and he took the road north again. Fine by her—she couldn't think of anything nicer than making love with him in that wonderful warm water again.

But he turned off on a side road well before he should. Then took another, a gravel road this time. The building appeared out of nowhere. One of those churches that had been built a century ago and now was stuck in the middle of a field with nothing else around—no other buildings, no cars, nothing.

'Sophy.'

He switched off the engine. He was so pale she was seriously worried.

'Lorenzo?'

He turned to face her. 'Will you marry me?' It was only once he'd asked it that he looked directly into her eyes.

She blinked, stunned at the question that had come so suddenly out of the blue. 'Yes. Of course I will.' Her heart thudded hard enough to burst from her chest.

But he didn't smile. Didn't look even a smidge more relaxed. He just jerked his head in a sharp negating gesture. 'But will you marry me right now?'

She stared from him, to the church in front of them. *'Now?'*

'Right now.' He sat still as marble.

'Of course I will.' She answered in a heartbeat.

'You're sure? You're absolutely sure?' He was the colour of marble too.

'Yes,' she said. 'But are you?'

He smiled then. It was as if the full power of the sun

had burst through the storm clouds—scattering them to the furthest edge of the universe. He got out of the car, strode round to her door and opened it.

She stepped out carefully, looking cautiously at him as he took her hand and led her to the closed doors of the old church.

'We can't really get married now can we?' She climbed the stairs doubtfully. She didn't think there was a minister in there—there wasn't a car in the yard, there didn't seem to be another soul around for miles.

Unless he meant to do some little personal made-up thing for just the two of them? Well, that would be fine by her. She wanted to be with him. She was happy.

He pulled the heavy door open and was a half-step behind her as she went in. She blinked in the dim light, suddenly saw the movement. The turning of heads. The smiles.

The church was full of people. *Full.*

She looked at Lorenzo—saw the colour had leeched from his skin again. A tall streak came flying up the aisle to her.

'Rosanna, what are you doing here?' Sophy asked, utterly shocked.

'I'm your bridesmaid, silly.'

'You're serious.' Sophy stared. 'You're not serious.'

'I'm dead serious,' said Rosanna.

'So did you mean it?' Lorenzo asked quietly. 'You'll marry me right now?'

'No, I need at least ten minutes with her first.' Rosanna again.

Sophy ignored Rosanna. Took a step closer to him, reached up on tiptoe and pressed her lips to his.

'Five minutes, okay?' He whispered, cupping her jaw. 'Don't be late.'

She saw the anxiety hidden not so deep in his eyes. 'I won't be.'

Rosanna dragged her by the hand out of the church and around the back to the vestry entrance. 'Didn't you hear the man? Five minutes is all we have.'

'You're not wearing black.' Sophy stared at her stupidly.

'It's a wedding, not a funeral.'

Sophy clapped her hand over her mouth to stop the crazed giggle bursting out.

'Ta da.' Rosanna held up the hanger.

Sophy's jaw dropped and she took a few steps closer. 'Where did you find it?'

Rosanna shrugged. 'Darling, I'm a buyer. I shop for a living—you know this.'

'But, Ro—'

'I know, even for me it's outstanding. Now strip.'

Rosanna held the dress for Sophy to step into. Fixing the zip for her and smoothing the skirt, holding the new shoes that were the exact shade to match.

'It all fits.'

'Of course. I am a professional.'

'Oh, Ro—'

'No getting emotional. Not yet,' Rosanna said tartly. 'Now, we can do a better job of hiding this bruise.' Despite her astringent tone, Rosanna swept the brush gently through Sophy's hair, quickly but carefully put in some clips. 'A rub of lipstick. You don't need any other make-up—you're glowing as it is.'

Sophy needed a distraction—otherwise she was going to hyperventilate, or get hysterical, or run into the church right now, half-ready, just to make sure it really was happening. She looked at her friend's demure French navy frock. 'Is Vance here?'

'Yes.'

Sophy glanced—that was an arctic-sounding answer. 'Are you not getting on?'

'We've never got on. We just got *it* on a few times.'

Yeah, but Sophy had suspected, just for a fleeting second, that maybe Rosanna had finally met her match. 'So what happened?'

'He told me I had to give up the others. It was him and no one else. An ultimatum, no less.'

'How unreasonable of him,' Sophy remarked dryly. 'What did you say?'

'I said no, of course.'

'Oh, Rosanna—'

'Be quiet or I'll spread lipstick all over your cheeks.' Rosanna looked down. 'You know me, Soph. I'm thrilled for you, I am. But you know the whole monogamous happy-ever-after thing isn't for me. The only time I'll ever walk down an aisle is right now, as your witness.'

'I know.' Sophy put her hand on her friend. 'And you know how much I love you for doing it for me.'

Rosanna shrugged, reverting back to snappy. 'It was fun spending Lorenzo's money.' She stood back and assessed her handiwork. 'Okay, you've got something old—the dress. Something new—the shoes. Now for something borrowed and something blue.' She looked sly, undid the clasp on the necklace she wore round her neck.

'Rosanna.' Sophy's heart melted even more.

'You have to wear it. He loves it on you.'

The necklace she'd made. 'I'm giving it back to you after.'

'Of course, it's borrowed.' Rosanna smiled. 'You look like you've put that stuff in your eyes. They're all big and sparkly.'

'Deadly nightshade?'

'Dad!' Sophy whirled around.

'You look beautiful.' He walked towards her, looking super-establishment in his grey suit. But he was smiling that wonderful, proud smile. 'Would you like me to walk up the aisle with you, Sophy?'

'Oh, Dad.' She took the two paces and he folded her into his arms. 'Just the one way.'

He laughed. 'Yes, you have the exit covered already.'

'How did this happen?' She couldn't believe it.

'Lorenzo's spent the last three days organising it.'

'But is it legal?'

'I'm a judge, honey. Of course it is.'

'But how?'

'He's a good man. And he knows how to get things done.'

Sophy nodded. 'He's very strong. He's wonderful to me.'

'I can see that. It's obvious how much he cares for you. A person who loves you like that, we'll always welcome.'

Sophy bit her lip. Did Lorenzo love her? In his own way she knew he must—he'd never be doing this otherwise. And maybe one day he'd even be able to tell her.

Her mother came to the door. 'Hurry up, the poor boy is out there looking paler than a ghost.'

The poor boy? Sophy choked back the laughing sob and gave her mother a hug.

'No tears, you two,' her father said gruffly. 'You'll both ruin your make-up.'

'Hold it together, Renz. She won't be a minute.'

'I won't be happy until it's done.' Until she was his. He breathed out a long breath—trying to control the racing pulse, the nerves slowly killing him. 'Thanks for being here.'

'I wouldn't have missed this for the world. Dani is beside herself with excitement. You should have heard her on the flight—"I can't believe it, I can't believe it" over and over.'

'I'm sure you figured out a way to shut her up.' Lorenzo flicked a quick glance to where his friend's wife sat sandwiched between Kat and Cara, who had her new baby cuddled to her breast. They were out of the neo-natal unit and thriving. Her husband looked like a doting fool. Lorenzo went even more tense—could barely dare hope that he'd be like that one day. His attention swerved straight back to the door at the back of the church. Where was she? Had this all been a huge mistake? Was she working out a way of backing out of it without embarrassing him?

'Relax.'

Easy for Alex to say. But Sophy was his one hope of salvation. The link to the vulnerable humanity he knew he'd hidden away a long time ago. But with her he had the courage—and the desire—to open up and be everything. To do everything. To embrace all that life had to offer.

He cleared his throat. Okay, so maybe the courage bit was fading. He needed to see her. Had he done the right thing? Her whole family was here. All thirty thousand of them. There was music all of a sudden and an expectant hush descended. The whole congregation stood for her.

Lorenzo couldn't remember the last time he'd cried. Decades ago probably, as a kid getting a hiding. But the lump in his throat now was like a burning ball of metal— only instead of melting it was getting harder and harder and bigger.

He staved off the tears by sheer will—based in the raw desire to see her clearly at this moment. No stupid salty water blurring the vision of her walking to meet him. Man, she was beautiful. The dress was white and slim fitting and frothed to the floor. Her blue eyes, almost painfully bright, looked nowhere but right into him.

She smiled. And his heart burst open.

He followed the minister's instructions—repeated the words, listened to her cool, clear voice say them back to him.

So he could kiss her now. But there was something he needed to do first—here and now and in front of a hundred witnesses.

He cleared his throat, took a deep breath as he turned to face her, gazing right into her beautiful blue eyes.

And finally he said it—the thing he'd never said to anyone before. Had never dreamed he'd ever be capable of saying, let alone actually feeling.

'I love you.' Suddenly he was freed from the terrible tension he'd felt for ever. 'I love you.' He said it again with a smile—louder that time as he recognised it as the beginning of a whole new meaning to his life.

She crumpled and he caught her to him, tasting her tears as he kissed her.

He did. He really did love her—the power of it was beyond anyone's control. Certainly his. But that was okay. That was better than okay.

Sophy heard him whispering it again as he held her in a bear hug so tight she couldn't breathe. But she wasn't letting him get away with just one kiss. Not after that. She put her palms on his face, blinking through the tears, feeling her soul sing as she touched her lips to his. She was tight in his arms again, literally swept off her feet as they kissed.

There was cheering and clapping and, for her, utter reluctance as they drew apart. Sophy turned, faced the sea of smiles and sparkling outfits for only a second. Then she turned back to him and was centred again. He was her anchor. And she his. Together they'd form a foundation from which they could do anything.

He kissed her again, the way she needed to be kissed—with love and heat and fierce intensity.

'I love you, Lorenzo.'

He smiled, that rare, shining, carefree smile that she hoped would now be much more common.

She'd known there were people. As she'd walked up the aisle she'd seen them in her peripheral vision. But all her attention had been on the man waiting for her at the altar. Stock-still, pale, looking at her as if she were an illusion—as if fearful she'd disappear in a wisp of smoke if he so much as blinked.

Now, as they walked back down the aisle together, her arm tightly clamped to his side, she saw them all properly—her parents, her brother and sister, aunts, a few cousins, Rosanna's boys, several other friends. And she recognised the Wilsons, Vance, Kat, Cara, some others who she guessed were vineyard workers. All were here to celebrate with them.

From somewhere—who knew where?—a couple of large buses had appeared out the front of the church. They all climbed aboard and were taken to the reception in a marquee in the middle of the Wilsons' vineyard. They dined and danced and laughed. It seemed Lorenzo really had impressed her father. The two of them bonded over fine wine and possible investments. Her mother was just floored by him. Sophy understood that all too well. Sophy gazed round at the gleaming silverware, the white and silver decorations making the room sparkle.

It was the grandest gesture anyone had ever done for her. She who'd organised this and that—the surprise parties here, the celebrations there. The biggest day of her life had been arranged by all who loved her. In an old church in the middle of nowhere the man she loved had given himself to her—unreservedly.

'I can't believe you did this for me.' She gazed up at him as they danced together on the specially constructed wooden floor.

'I wanted to do something nice for you.' He smiled faintly.

'You've done a lot of nice things already, Lorenzo—you gave me workshop space, you gave me time in Hanmer, you did those designs for me.'

'But it was all with conditions. There are no conditions on this.'

'Other than that I promise to be your wife and to love you always.'

'Just that little thing, yeah.'

'Unconditionally given.'

He pulled her closer. 'Do you mind not getting to organise your own wedding?'

'Mind?' She laughed. 'I'm so relieved I don't have to. No stress. I could just enjoy it.'

'Rosanna was fantastic.' He brushed her cheek with the backs of his fingers. 'So were your parents.'

'Thank you so much.'

'They love you.'

She nodded, unable to speak any more.

'Sophy?'

She turned into his arms, hiding her tears in his neck.

'I love you.'

She looked at him then. He was smiling, his face light, his eyes warm and free of shadows. 'If I'd known how good it felt to say it, I'd have said it back that day when you rang for the doctor in my apartment. I wanted to make love to you then—I'm going to now.'

She reached up to him, placing the palm of her hand on

the slightly rough cheek. 'Thank goodness,' she sighed. 'I was worried you'd taken a vow of abstinence.'

'I did,' he said soberly. 'I wasn't going to be with you again until you were my wife.'

'And now I am.'

'Yes.'

They whispered quiet goodbyes to the others, then slipped away in the night—running together down the rows of vines, to the small cottage at the far corner of the land. It had been decked in flowers, the sweet scent filling the air.

His arms were tight about her. 'Thank you, thank you, thank you.'

'For what?'

'Everything.' He looked down, a half-smile quirking his lips. 'I talked to your father.'

'You did?' She felt some nerves twinge.

'When I asked him for his blessing. It was a pretty frank talk.' He looked rueful. 'But he reckoned it's impossible to control feelings or to stop them, but that it's better to accept them. And then to deal with them.' He laced his fingers through hers. 'I want to deal with my love for you. Now and every day to come.'

And then he did—showing her the tenderness she'd made him feel, the happiness she'd brought to life in him. She cried as he told her, showed her, loved her. And she held him, loved him, until he shook in her arms.

'Not alone,' she whispered. 'Not any more.'

He buried his hot face in her neck and she stroked him until both their tears were spent.

'Are we staying here?' She was finally back on earth and able to absorb something of her surroundings.

'For a few days.'

'Then why do you have my passport?'

He chuckled. 'So you couldn't say no and run away overseas.'

'I'd only want to run away with you.'

'And we will. Very soon. But I thought we could decide where together.' He twirled her hair round his finger. 'You're tired.'

She was. But so happy. She snuggled closer to him and discovered she wasn't *that* tired. 'Once was not enough, Lorenzo.'

'Demanding wench.' He rose onto his elbow. 'You're always asking me for more.'

She laughed. 'And isn't it just such a hardship for you?'

'No,' he said, pulling her closer, binding her in his arms. 'It's heaven.'

Pure heaven.

Coming Next Month

from **Harlequin Presents® EXTRA.** Available February 8, 2011.

Coming Next Month

from **Harlequin Presents®.** Available February 22, 2011.

REQUEST YOUR
FREE BOOKS!

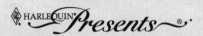

2 FREE NOVELS PLUS
2 FREE GIFTS!

YES! Please send me 2 FREE Harlequin Presents® novels and my 2 FREE gifts (gifts are worth about $10). After receiving them, if I don't wish to receive any more books, I can return the shipping statement marked "cancel." If I don't cancel, I will receive 6 brand-new novels every month and be billed just $4.05 per book in the U.S. or $4.74 per book in Canada. That's a saving of at least 15% off the cover price! It's quite a bargain! Shipping and handling is just 50¢ per book.* I understand that accepting the 2 free books and gifts places me under no obligation to buy anything. I can always return a shipment and cancel at any time. Even if I never buy another book, the two free books and gifts are mine to keep forever.

106/306 HDN E5M4

Name	(PLEASE PRINT)

Address	Apt. #

City	State/Prov.	Zip/Postal Code

Signature (if under 18, a parent or guardian must sign)

Mail to the **Harlequin Reader Service:**
IN U.S.A.: P.O. Box 1867, Buffalo, NY 14240-1867
IN CANADA: P.O. Box 609, Fort Erie, Ontario L2A 5X3

Not valid for current subscribers to Harlequin Presents books.

Are you a current subscriber to Harlequin Presents books and want to receive the larger-print edition? Call 1-800-873-8635 today!

* Terms and prices subject to change without notice. Prices do not include applicable taxes. N.Y. residents add applicable sales tax. Canadian residents will be charged applicable provincial taxes and GST. Offer not valid in Quebec. This offer is limited to one order per household. All orders subject to approval. Credit or debit balances in a customer's account(s) may be offset by any other outstanding balance owed by or to the customer. Please allow 4 to 6 weeks for delivery. Offer available while quantities last.

Your Privacy: Harlequin Books is committed to protecting your privacy. Our Privacy Policy is available online at www.eHarlequin.com or upon request from the Reader Service. From time to time we make our lists of customers available to reputable third parties who may have a product or service of interest to you. If you would prefer we not share your name and address, please check here. ☐

Help us get it right—We strive for accurate, respectful and relevant communications. To clarify or modify your communication preferences, visit us at www.ReaderService.com/consumerschoice.

USA TODAY *bestselling author Lynne Graham*
is back with a thrilling new trilogy
SECRETLY PREGNANT, CONVENIENTLY WED

Three heroines must marry alpha males to keep
their dreams…but Alejandro, Angelo and Cesario
are not about to be tamed!

Book 1—JEMIMA'S SECRET
Available March 2011 from Harlequin Presents®.

JEMIMA yanked open a drawer in the sideboard to find
Alfie's birth certificate. Her son was her husband's child.
It was a question of telling the truth whether she liked it or
not. She extended the certificate to Alejandro.

"This has to be nonsense," Alejandro asserted.

"Well, if you can find some other way of explaining how
I managed to give birth by that date and Alfie not be yours,
I'd like to hear it," Jemima challenged.

Alejandro glanced up, golden eyes bright as blades and
as dangerous. "All this proves is that you must still have
been pregnant when you walked out on our marriage. It
does not automatically follow that the child is mine."

"'I know it doesn't suit you to hear this news now and I
really didn't want to tell you. But I can't lie to you about it.
Someday Alfie may want to look you up and get acquainted."

"If what you have just told me is the truth, if that little
boy does prove to be mine, it was vindictive and extremely
selfish of you to leave me in ignorance!"

Jemima paled. "When I left you, I had no idea that I was
still pregnant."

"Two years is a long period of time, yet you made no
attempt to inform me that I might be a father. I will want
DNA tests to confirm your claim before I make any deci-

sion about what I want to do."

"Do as you like," she told him curtly. "*I* know who Alfie's father is and there has never been any doubt of his identity."

"I will make arrangements for the tests to be carried out and I will see you again when the result is available," Alejandro drawled with lashings of dark Spanish masculine reserve.

"I'll contact a solicitor and start the divorce," Jemima proffered in turn.

Alejandro's eyes narrowed in a piercing scrutiny that made her uncomfortable. "It would be foolish to do anything before we have that DNA result."

"I disagree," Jemima flashed back. "I should have applied for a divorce the minute I left you!"

Alejandro quirked an ebony brow. "And why didn't you?"

Jemima dealt him a fulminating glance but said nothing, merely moving past him to open her front door in a blunt invitation for him to leave.

"I'll be in touch," he delivered on the doorstep.

What is Alejandro's next move? Perhaps rekindling their marriage is the only solution! But will Jemima agree?

Find out in Lynne Graham's
exciting new romance
JEMIMA'S SECRET

Available March 2011
from Harlequin Presents®.

Start your Best Body today with these top 3 nutrition tips!

1. **SHOP THE PERIMETER OF THE GROCERY STORE:** The good stuff—fruits, veggies, lean proteins and dairy—always line the outer edges of the store. When you veer into the center aisles, you enter the temptation zone, where the unhealthy foods live.

2. **WATCH PORTION SIZES:** Most portion sizes in restaurants are nearly twice the size of a true serving and at home, it's easy to "clean your plate." Use these easy serving guidelines:
   - Protein: the palm of your hand
   - Grains or Fruit: a cup of your hand
   - Veggies: the palm of two open hands

3. **USE THE RAINBOW RULE FOR PRODUCE:** Your produce drawers should be filled with every color of fruits and vegetables. The greater the variety, the more vitamins and other nutrients you add to your diet.

Find these and many more helpful tips in